英文文法沒這麼難

The Journey of Self-discovery

許貴運 ◎著

我靠哲學名句 找回學文法的勇氣

Courage is knowing what not to fear. —Plato
勇氣就是知道不該害怕的是什麼。—柏拉圖
A journey of a thousand miles begins with a single step. —Lao Tzu
千里之行,始於足下。—老子

哲學名句:以文法主題為主軸輔以充斥於生活中的東、西方哲學名句,能**沉澱思緒**、**激發思考力**與**寫作靈感**。

名句故事:收錄哲學家背景故事,可從中汲取哲學家的人生智慧,同步提升自我涵養跟英文寫作的內容**深度**跟**廣度**,重新定義你的生活態度。

句型文法解析:從名句中延伸出文法解析,以更全面、多元的方式學習文法,能靈活轉換句式,達到**自我檢視**跟**強化學習**的功效。

英文例句:每句例句均以幽默、詼諧的口吻寫成,能強化學習與記憶,以事半功倍的方式獲取寫作佳績。

　　哲學可以讓人變得更有智慧，但相關書籍常常比較難懂，所以不少人因而卻步。我們選了一些經典的哲學名句，讓讀者在最短的時間內得到最大的收穫，不但英文有所長進，也增長一些智慧。

　　這本書比較特別之處是除了西方哲學名句外，也介紹一些中國哲學名句，像是老子和莊子哲學，還有孔子和孟子學說。以老子為例，所談的道理雖然很簡單，卻蘊藏著很大的智慧。譬如：在「以其終不自為大，故能成其大」這句話中，老子教導我們不自以為偉大才能變得偉大的道理，翻成英文則是"Making no claim to greatness leads to greatness."英文翻譯以動名詞作為主詞，除了帶出該單元所要介紹的文法概念外，也用最簡潔的方式來表達一個哲學概念。

　　本書的目的就是藉由哲學名句來讓讀者輕鬆地學英文，「名句故事」是根據哲學名句所做的解釋或闡釋，文法概念則在介紹哲學名句所牽涉到的句型、字詞、或文法，例句部分是用比較長的句子來說明如何活用。

許貴運

時至今日，仍舊有許多哲學家的至理名言流傳著，如果能透過哲學家的名言，帶出文法概念，那麼學習肯定能更輕鬆、快樂！

本書共收錄了12位東、西方哲學家說過的名句，包含希臘三哲蘇格拉底、柏拉圖、亞里斯多德；西方哲學家笛卡兒、培根、尼采、康德；東方儒家的孔子、孟子、荀子；道家的老子、莊子。每單元皆藉由引述的名句，延伸出文法概念解析，並在每個單元後提供例句，幫助讀者更曉得該如何活用文法。

請一起跟著本書踏入哲學和英文文法融合的世界吧！謝謝乃文老師的用心！

編輯部

Contents 目次

PART 2 · 西方哲思：我思故我在

PART 3 · 儒家思想：人之初，性本善？性本惡？

PART 4 · 老莊思想：道可道，非常道

1 希臘三哲：

吾愛吾師，吾更愛真理

 the + adj. / V.ing / p.p

🏛 哲學名句

The unexamined life is not worth living. ——*Socrates*

未經檢驗的人生不值得去過。——蘇格拉底

📖 名句故事

"The unexamined life is not worth living" is a famous statement made by Socrates at his trial for corrupting the minds of young Athens and impiety, for which he was later sentenced to death by drinking poison.

An "unexamined life" refers to a life without philosophy. Philosophy, the love of wisdom, is the most important art or occupation for Socrates.

It is a pursuit of wisdom through questioning and logical thinking, which can be summed up in one word: examining. Only in the process of self-examination can one understand the meaning of life. We have to thank Socrates for giving us ways to live a meaningful life.

「未經檢驗的人生不值得去過」是蘇格拉底的名言，他在因污染雅典年輕人心靈及不虔誠罪名而受審時説下這句話，稍後他被處以死刑，喝下毒藥身亡。

「未經檢驗的人生」指的是缺乏哲學的人生。哲學是愛好智慧之意，對蘇格拉底來説是最重要的藝術或工作。

哲學經由質疑和邏輯思考來追求智慧，總結來説就是：檢視。只有在自我檢視的過程中才能瞭解生命的意義。我們必須感謝蘇格拉底給了我們過有意義生活的方式。

句型文法解析

哲學例句中的 **unexamined** 是過去分詞作為形容詞用，意思是「未經檢驗的」，我們來個腦筋急轉彎，原句是「未經檢驗的人生不值得去過」，可以改成 **The examined life is worth living.**（經過檢驗的人生值得去過）。

這一單元介紹的就是分詞形容詞，分詞可分現在分詞和過去分詞，現在分詞是在動詞的字尾加上ing，用於現在進行式，過去分詞則是在動詞的字尾加上ed，用於完成式和被動語態。

分詞形容詞是指擺在名詞之前修飾該名詞或作為主詞補語之用的現在分詞或過去分詞，主要是由 interest、bore、excite、surprise、tire、touch 等情緒動詞演變而成：interested / interesting、bored / boring、excited / exciting、surprised / surprising、tired / tiring、touched / touching。這類形容詞通常是過去分詞當主詞補語，現在分詞則作為修飾名詞的形容詞之用，例如：I am interested in the book.（我對這本書很有興趣。）/ It is an interesting book.（這是一本有趣的書。）切記不能説 It is an interested book，不過 interesting 也能用作主詞補語，像是 The book is interesting to me. 但可不能説 The book is interested to me. 這類形容詞的用法大致上依循此規則，過去分詞表達人的情緒，現在分詞則表達事情或物件給人的感覺。

同類形容詞還有 confused / confusing、embarrassed / embarrassing、frightened / frightening。此外，這類過去分詞形

容詞後面會接介系詞形成一個片語：be interested in、be excited about、be surprised at、be bored with、be tired of、be embarrassed at、be confused about、be frightened at。

英文例句

接著就來看看分詞形容詞可以怎樣應用到句子中吧！

✡ **An interesting book** is a book that interests the reader while **a boring book** is a book that bores the reader.
有趣的書是吸引讀者的書，而無聊的書則是讓讀者感到無聊的書。

✡ As learning English, most students **are confused about** the spelling of certain words, such as leisure and neighbor, which they often misspell because their pronunciation is a little bit difficult.
學習英文時，多數學生對leisure和neighbor之類字的拼法感到困惑，這些字的發音方式讓學生經常拼錯。

✡ We wouldn't **be surprised** if we were visited by aliens someday.
如果有天外星人造訪地球，我們不會感到驚訝。

2 of N.

The only true wisdom is in knowing you know nothing.

——Socrates

真正的智慧是在於知道自己的無知。——蘇格拉底

名句**故事**

What Socrates is saying is that the only thing he knows is that he knows nothing. He wants us to be humble. It is not easy.

People tend to pretend to know everything when they know only a little bit of everything. As the saying goes, empty vessels make the most sound.

Don't be a shallow person. Keep your mind humble and open to new knowledge. It is easy for us to become a proud person who likes to brag about who he is, what he has done, and where he has been. A humble person is easy to get along with. He learns from others. That's how he gains wisdom.

蘇格拉底的意思是，他唯一知道的事情是他的無知。他要我們謙卑，這並不容易。

人們通常會假裝知道所有事情，其實他們只是每樣東西都知道一點。如俗諺所云，半瓶水響叮噹。

不要做一個膚淺的人，讓你的心胸謙卑並開放容納新的知識。我們很容易成為一個驕傲的人，喜歡吹噓自己是誰、做過什麼事情、及去過哪裡。謙虛的人很好相處，他向其他人學習。那是他獲得智慧的方法。

句型文法解析

哲學名句也可說成 The only thing **of importance** is knowing you know nothing.（唯一重要的事是知道自己的無知），原句中的 knowing 前面有 in，改寫的句子則不需要 in。

在介系詞 of 後面加上名詞可以構成一個相當於形容詞的片語，最常見的是 of importance，意思就是 important。例如：But what is of great importance to me is observation of the movement of colors. —Robert Delaunay（但對我很重要的是觀察色彩的律動。—法國藝術家羅伯特・德勞），從這句可以看到 what is of great importance to me 就等於 what is greatly important to me，你們或許會問，為什麼要這麼麻煩？

英文是一個講究修辭的語言，經常用不同的字或詞語來表達同一個概念，所以才會有那麼多同義字，但就算同義字也不是意思上完全相同，這是有趣的地方。除了 of importance 外，其他類似的片語還有 of significance (significant)、of value (valuable)、of use (useful)、of help (helpful)、of courage (courageous) 等。

這類片語除了可以作為主詞補語外，也可放在名詞後面修飾名詞，例如：He is a man of importance. (He is an important man.)；a matter of significance (a significant matter)。

通常可以在片語中的名詞之前加個形容詞，用來表達程度，像是 a man of some importance 和 a matter of significance，意思是

有點重要，重要程度反而比不上未加形容詞 some 之前。孫子的名言「是故上攻伐　」被翻成：Thus, what is of supreme importance in war is to attack the enemy's strategy.

🏅 **英文例句**

接著就來看看 of N. 可以怎樣應用到句子中吧！

✡ He is a man **of courage** who doesn't run away, but remains at his post and fights against the enemy.
他是一個有勇氣之人，不會逃之夭夭，而會堅守崗位與敵人奮戰到底。

✡ A man **of value** is not necessarily a man of success since the former brings value to other people, while the latter cares more about himself.
有價值的人不見得是成功的人，因為前者為他人帶來價值，而後者比較關心自己。

✡ Eating well is a matter **of great importance** because we are what we eat.
吃得很是一件很重要的事，因為我們吃什麼就變成什麼。

3 ▶ N1 of a(n) N2

哲學名句

There is only one good, knowledge, and one evil, ignorance.——*Socrates*

只有一種善，那就是知識；只有一種惡，那就是無知。

——蘇格拉底

名句故事

As we all know, knowledge is power. It is a good in itself. It gives us the ability to think. By contrast, ignorance is a lack of knowledge. It can lead us to make wrong choices. It is linked to prejudice and many other things that make us become unwelcome.

A man of knowledge is a knowledgeable man, while an ignorant man is a man without knowledge. What really matters is not what we take in but what we give out.

Knowledge is something that we can give out. That's why we need knowledge. An ignorant man has nothing to give out unless he is rich enough to share his money with other people.

我們都知道，知識就是力量。知識本身就是一種善，讓我們有思考的能力。反之，無知就是缺乏知識，會讓我們做出錯誤選擇。和無知相關的是偏見及其他許多使我們不受歡迎的事情。

有知識的人是個知識豐富的人，而無知的人則是沒有知識的人。真正重要的不是我們拿了什麼東西，而是給了什麼東西。

知識是我們可以給的東西，那是我們為何需要知識的原因。無知的人沒有什麼東西可以給，除非他有錢到足以與其他人分享他的金錢。

句型文法解析

　　根據哲學名句，我們可以衍伸出這樣的句子：A man of knowledge can do good things, while a man of ignorance can do bad things without knowing that they are bad things.（有知識的人可以做好事，而無知的人卻可以做壞事而不自知）。這就帶出我們這一單元要介紹的文法概念之一，即 of+抽象名詞所構成的形容詞片語。

　　知名美國語言學家愛德華‧沙皮爾（Edward Sapir）曾說：One of the glories of English simplicity is the possibility of using the same word as noun and verb.（英文簡單所具有的最大亮點之一是可以用同一個字來做名詞和動詞之用）。這個句子的主詞是 one of the glories of English simplicity，其結構是用兩個介系詞 of 連接了 one、the glories、及 English simplicity，這個單元要介紹的就是這種用 of 連結兩個名詞或名詞片語的文法結構。

　　這種結構很常見，像是 the roof of a church（教堂的屋頂）、the head of a family（家長）、the leader of a class（班長）、the president of a country（總統），這幾個例子都在表達從屬關係。

　　另一種是同位格關係：the city of New York（也可說成 New York City）、the art of painting（或 the painting art）、the problem of air pollution（或 the air pollution problem）。

還有修飾的關係：a man of importance（an important man）、a man of ability（an able man）。

另一種是表示物質名詞的形狀、容器、及單位：a piece of paper、a slice of bread、a bottle of milk、two glasses of water、a cup of tea、a pound of sugar。

英文例句

接著就來看看 N1 of a(n) N2 可以怎樣應用到句子中吧！

✡ If you are thirsty, there are **a glass of water** and **a bottle of milk** on the table.
如果你口渴，桌上有一杯水和一瓶牛奶。

✡ **The President of the United States** is often considered to be the most powerful man in the world, yet it might not necessarily be true.
美國總統通常被認為是世界上最有權力的人，但或許不一定是真的。

✡ **The city of New York** is a leading business center in the U.S. and a destination for immigrants from around the world.
紐約市是美國一個主要商業中心及世界各國移民鎖定的目的地。

4 What... for?

哲學名句

Wonder is the beginning of wisdom. ——*Socrates*

驚奇是智慧的開端。——蘇格拉底

名句故事

When we wonder about something, we become interested in it, which is the beginning of a learning process. Wisdom is gained through learning.

When you are wonderstruck by something, you have the feeling of wonder and the desire to know something about it. That's why wonder is the beginning of wisdom. Wonder is equivalent to a feeling of "wow" toward something.

When you feel wowed about a song or anything that catches your interest instantly, you want to keep that feeling. You may choose to listen to the song again and again. In doing so, you begin to learn something from the song, the value of which you may not be able to understand until sometime later. When you understand it, you become wiser.

當我們對某樣事物感到驚奇時，就會對它有興趣，那就是一個學習過程的開端。智慧是經由學習取得。

當你對某件事物感到驚奇萬分時，你有了驚奇之感及想要瞭解它的慾望。那是驚奇何以成為智慧開端的原因。驚奇相當於對某件事物感到「哇」。

當你對一首歌或任何即刻引起你興趣的事物感到哇時，你想要維持那種感覺。你或許會選擇反覆聽那首歌，這樣一來你就從歌曲中學習到某些東西，你或許稍後才理解其價值。等到你理解的那一刻，你就變得更有智慧一點。

句型文法解析

哲學名句 Wonder is the beginning of wisdom.（驚奇是智慧的開端）其實意思類似於 What wonder stands for is the beginning of wisdom.（驚奇代表的是智慧的開端）。本單元介紹的就是 what...for 的用法。

1980 年代著名歌 "That's What Friends Are For"《朋友之道》曾經膾炙人口，曲名裡有本單元要介紹的 what...for。That's what friends are for 的意思是朋友之所以為朋友的理由。

what...for 可用於直述句或疑問句中，直述句中 what 和 for 通常會拆開來，for 擺句尾。疑問句中 what 和 for 有拆開來的，也有不拆開來的。例如：What did you do that for? 或 For what did you do that? / A: I am going to Taipei tomorrow. B: What for?（去做什麼？）或 For what?（為什麼？）

從這些例句看出，what 和 for 在疑問句中可以分開來或合在一起，意思都一樣，而作為反問的疑問詞時，則要連在一起，不是 what for 就是 for what，但兩者意思不太一樣，如前面的例句所示。

what for 或 for what 雖然都有類似 why 的意思，但 why 就是單純地問理由，比較不會夾雜著一些額外的意思。

　　當你用 what for 問某人時，你有點在質疑他做某件事情的意義，所以還是用 why 比較保險，但學習英文還是應該知道 what for 和 for what 的用法，畢竟出現的機率還是挺高的。

英文例句

接著就來看看 What... for?可以怎樣應用到句子中吧！

✡ When you say "**What's that for?**", you actually mean "Why's that?"

當你說「那是怎樣？」時，你實際上的意思是「為何是那樣？」

✡ We all know what money is for, but we may not necessarily know what money is or **what it stands for**.

我們都知道錢要做什麼，卻不一定知道錢是什麼或錢代表什麼。

✡ A: **What did you say that for**? B: I said that to make you understand that you made a mistake and that you needed to be aware of it.

A: 你為何那樣說？ B：我那樣說的目的是讓你瞭解你犯了錯誤，必須意識到錯在哪裡。

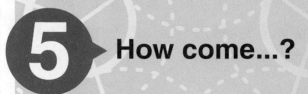

5 ▶ How come...?

‖‖‖ 哲學名句

Strong minds discuss ideas, average minds discuss events, weak minds discuss people. ——*Socrates*

強者討論理念，庸者討論事件，弱者討論他人。——蘇格拉底

名句故事

There is much truth to the maxim. It is not easy to understand it, however. Take a news event as an example. Weak minds pay attention to people involved in the event, while average minds heed the event itself. Only strong minds discuss the underlying causes of the event. Does that ring a bell to you?

A tabloid newspaper always highlights celebrities' private lives, while a serious newspaper cares more about social and political issues.

It takes a lot of time and effort to be a great mind. In the same way, you need to study hard to get high test scores and be admitted into a good university.

這句格言有諸多真理,可是不太容易瞭解。以一個新聞事件為例,弱者只關注事件中的人物,庸者關注事件本身,只有強者才探討事件的背後成因。這樣瞭嗎?

八卦報紙總是以名人的私生活為重點,而嚴肅的報紙則比較關心社會和政治議題。

成為強者要花許多的時間和努力。同樣的,你要努力讀書才能考試得高分並進入好的大學就讀。

句型文法解析

哲學名句陳述一種看法，我們則可據此提出疑問，即 How come strong minds discuss ideas and weak minds discuss people? 這個問句形式是本單元要介紹的。

how come 這個片語本來屬於口語用法，不能用在正式的書寫文章中，但現在由於使用者漸多，地位隨之水漲船高，已不再被視為不登大雅之堂。

how come 的意思就是「怎麼」和「為什麼」，相當於 why，但不完全等於，因為 why 是客觀地問原因，而 how come 則帶有疑惑的意味，表示怎麼會這樣。例如：Why do you look so tired today? 表示你為什麼今天看起來這麼疲倦？而 How come you look so tired today? 則表示你怎麼今天看起來這麼疲倦？

用法：how come 雖然出現在疑問句中，但後面的句型不用倒裝，也不用考慮添加助動詞的問題，用法很簡單，難怪越來越受歡迎。

例句：If evolution really works, how come mothers only have two hands?（如果進化真的發揮作用，怎麼媽媽還是只有兩隻手？）

If truth is beauty, how come no one has their hair done in a library.（如果真理就是美，怎麼沒人在圖書館裡做頭髮？）

If Jesus was a Jew, how come he has a Mexican first name?（如果耶穌是猶太人，怎麼他有一個墨西哥名字？）

最後一個例句需要解釋一下，所謂墨西哥名字應該是指西班牙名字，Jesus 是西班牙名字，中文翻成黑素斯，網路上不是有個叫做黑素斯的西班牙人嗎？

英文例句

接著就來看看 How come...?可以怎樣應用到句子中吧！

✡ If you really want to study abroad after graduating from college, **how come** you waste your time on playing video games all day long?

如果你真的想要在大學畢業後到國外念書，怎麼整天把時間浪費在打電腦遊戲上？

✡ **How come** I forget things so easily as I am under great job stress?

為什麼我在工作壓力很大時很容易忘記事情？

✡ **How come** horses sleep standing up, while many other land animals can lie down and fall into a deep sleep like humans?

為什麼馬站著睡覺，而許多其他陸上動物卻能像人類一樣躺下來進入深層睡眠？

6 How / What about + N. / V.ing

Ⅲ 哲學名句

Education is the kindling of a flame, not the filling of a vessel. ——*Socrates*

教育是點燃火焰，而不是裝填容器。——蘇格拉底

名句故事

The kindling of a flame means to enlighten students with ideas, while the filling of a vessel refers to dumping a large amount of information into students' minds. They represent two different ways of education.

The former way of teaching requires teachers to inspire students, while the latter treats students as empty vessels that need to be filled with as much knowledge as possible.

Education is about helping students develop curiosity for knowledge. Students should not be treated like containers passively waiting to be filled with knowledge. But it is not easy for a teacher to enlighten students with ideas. They have to keep on learning as well.

點燃火焰的意思是用思想啟發學生，而裝填容器是指把大量的資訊塞到學生的腦袋裡。它們代表兩種不同的教育方式。

前者需要老師去啟發學生，後者則把學生當成需要被填入大量知識的空瓶罐。

教育是在幫助學生發展對知識的好奇，不該把學生當成被動地等待接收知識的容器。但要老師用思想啟發學生並不容易，他們也要不斷學習才行。

句型文法解析

哲學名句説 Education is the kindling of a flame，意思是教育是在點燃學生的求知火焰，而面對 What about instruction?（教學則是如何？）這個問題，我們可以回答説：Instruction is the filling of a vessel.

有一首英文歌叫做 "What about now?"《現在該如何？》，歌名用到了 what about，意思是「如何」，通常可以和 how about 相互替換，意思都是一樣。

例如：How / what about going to the movie?（去看電影如何？）這是在表達一種提議，What do you say to going to the movie? 也是一樣的意思。How / what about 及 what do say to 後面接名詞、代名詞、及動名詞。

例句：How about some apple pie?（來點蘋果派如何？）
I am fine. How about you?（我很好，你呢？）
A: We have Chinese, science, and art. What about you? B: We have English and P.E.（A: 我們有中文課、科學課、及美術課，你呢？B: 我們有英文課和體育課。）
A: How have been you? B: Good. How about you?（A: 近來如何？B: 很好，你呢？）

要特別注意的是，how / what about 後面也可以接一個完整的句子，例如：How about we clean the house tomorrow?

這是一個文法正確的句子，不過通常只要說成 How about cleaning the house tomorrow?就好。

前面提過的 How about going to the movie?也可說成 How about we go to the movie?

英文例句

接著就來看看 How / What about (What do you say to) + N. / V.ing 可以怎樣應用到句子中吧！

✡ **What about a cup of tea** with some snacks in our beautiful garden?
到我們美麗的花園喝杯茶吃些點心如何？

✡ **How about taking a day off** to make preparations for the upcoming charity activity for the poor people in our community?
休一天假來準備即將為我們社區的窮困人士舉行的慈善活動如何？

✡ **What do you say to renting a car** to travel around Taiwan and spending the night in the car during the tour without checking in at a hotel?
租台車環島旅行並在旅行期間不睡旅館改睡車上如何？

Wh- + to V

🏛 哲學名句

Wise men speak because they have something to say;

Fools because they have to say something.

——Plato

智者發言是因為有東西要說；愚者發言是因為要說些東西。

——柏拉圖

📖 名句故事

Plato means that wise men speak only when they have something to say. Fools speak only because they want to say something.

We can always find people who love to talk about trivial things or gossip about others. You can't discuss serious issues with these people. They don't consider themselves to be fools, yet they do look like fools to people who aren't interested in what they are talking about.

Wise men talk only when they have some thoughts to share with others. They are more concerned about issues such as the meaning of life and the pursuit of happiness. If they don't have anything to say, they won't talk only for the sake of talking.

柏拉圖的意思是，智者只要在有東西要説時才發言，愚者發言只是為了説點東西。

我們總是能找到喜歡談瑣碎事情或論他人是非的人，你無法和這些人討論嚴肅的事情。他們不認為自己是愚者，然對他們所説話題不感興趣的人來説，他們確實看起來像是愚者。

智者只有當有想法與他人分享時才發言，他們比較關心的是生命的意義和追求快樂之類議題。如果他們沒有事情要説，就不會為了發言而發言。

句型文法解析

根據哲學名句，我們可以衍生出這樣的句子：Wise men speak

as they know what to say, while fools speak even if they don't know what to say.（智者發言是因為知道要說些什麼，而愚者則是即便不知道要說什麼也會發言）。

　　What to do when you don't know what to do. 這個句子的意思是「當你不知道要做什麼時該做什麼」，既然不知要做什麼，又怎麼會知道該怎麼辦？此時就要請教有智慧的長者或老師，他們可以指點迷津。本單元介紹的是疑問詞+to 不定詞，**what to** 是一例，其他還有 **how to**、**who / whom to**、**where to**、**when to**。

　　這類慣用語是用來省略一個句子的其他部分，I don't know what to do. 是 I don't know what I should do. 的精簡說法，其他依此類推。

　　例如：He doesn't know how to swim.（他不知道怎麼游泳。）

　　I don't know where to go.（我不知道要去哪裡。）
等於 I don't know where I should go.

　　He doesn't know when to start.（他不知道哪時開始。）
等於 He doesn't know when he should start.

　　另外，whether 雖然不是疑問詞，但後面也可接 to 不定詞，例如：He can't decide whether to study abroad. 等於 He can't decide whether he should study abroad.（他無法決定他是否該出國留學。）

要注意的是，和 whether 意思和用法類似的 if，卻不能在後面接 to 不定詞，你如果要問為什麼，筆者的回答是，語言乃約定俗成之物，不見得一定有道理，只是因為經年累月所形成。

英文例句

接著就來看看 Wh- + to V 可以怎樣應用到句子中吧！

✳ If you don't know **what to do** next in life, just pack your backpack and go to a place where you can get rid of your worries.

如果你不知道在接下來的生命裡要做些什麼，就背上背包到一個你可以擺脫煩惱的地方。

✳ **How to start a new life** is a big issue that everyone is to be faced with sooner or later.

如何開始新生活是每個人或早或晚都會面對到的重大議題。

✳ He doesn't know **whether to take the job offer** since he already has a well-paid job.

他不知道是否該接受工作邀約，因為他已經有了一個待遇很好的工作。

2 Wh- + in the world / on earth

哲學名句

Music is a moral law. It gives soul to the universe, wings to the mind, flight to the imagination, and a charm to sadness, and life to everything. ——*Plato*

音樂是道德的律法，賦予宇宙靈魂，為頭腦帶來翅膀，讓想像力飛翔起來，使悲傷具有魔力，萬事萬物皆有生命。——柏拉圖

名句故事

Music played an important role in ancient Greece. We don't know what kind of music Plato was talking about. Good music is pleasing to the ear and soothing to the soul.

If you love classical music, you can understand what it means to give soul to the universe and wings to the mind.

Not everyone likes classical music, however. Many people love popular songs, which might not be Plato's cup of tea.

Popular songs could also give a charm to sadness and life to everything. What matters is that music is a moral law, which refers to a rule or group of rules conceived as universal and unchanging.

音樂在古希臘扮演著重要的角色。我們不曉得柏拉圖所提的是哪種音樂，好的音樂既悅耳動聽又撫慰心靈。

如果你喜歡古典音樂，就可以理解賦予宇宙靈魂及為頭腦帶來翅膀的意義。然而不是每個人都喜歡古典音樂，許多人喜歡流行歌曲，但那或許不對柏拉圖的胃。

流行歌曲也能使悲傷具有魔力及萬事萬物有了生命。重點是音樂是道德的律法，也就是被視為普遍和不變的一種規則或一組規則。

句型文法解析

　　根據哲學名句，我們可以衍生出這樣的句子：How on earth can music help us?（音樂到底可以幫我們什麼？）

　　當有人說 "What on earth do you mean?"，你可別以為他是說「你意思是地球上什麼東西？」他其實是說「你到底什麼意思？」

　　而 Who in the world do you think you are? 不是「你以為你是世界上的誰？」，而是「你到底以為你是誰？」

　　本單元介紹的是在 **what** 和 **who** 等疑問詞後面加上 **on earth** 和 **in the world** 等副詞，表達「究竟、到底」之意。

　　例如：
What on earth makes you say that?（到底是什麼讓你那麼說？）

　　Why on earth did she do that?（她到底為何那麼做？）

　　How on earth did you do it?（你到底怎麼做的？）

　　Who on earth would want to be your friend?（究竟誰會想當你的朋友？）

　　Where on earth did you see her?（你到底在哪裡看到她？）

加入 on earth 和 in the world 是為了加強語氣，類似的詞語還有 the hell、the devil、the heck，但這些詞語比較粗鄙，不太適合學生使用或學習，但知道一下也無妨。另外還有 ever、exactly、in God's name，但不是那麼常出現。

英文例句

接著就來看看 Wh- +in the world / on earth 可以怎樣應用到句子中吧！

✡ Do you know **what in the world** they are singing about? If you do, I'll really be surprised beyond measure.

你知道他們到底在唱什麼嗎？如果你知道，我真的會驚訝到無以名狀。

✡ **Who on earth** would help a man who always borrows money from his friends and seldom pays back money?

到底誰會幫一個老是跟朋友借錢卻很少還錢的人？

✡ **Where on earth** can scientists find a rare species that was spotted by a hiker in a mountain several months ago?

科學家到底可以在哪裡找到幾個月前被登山客在山裡發現的某種稀有物種？

3 ▶ It is... (for / of +sb.) + to V

IIII 哲學名句

We can easily forgive a child who is afraid of the dark; the real tragedy of life is when men are afraid of the light.

——Plato

我們可以輕易地原諒小孩的怕黑，生命真正的悲哀是當大人都害怕光明的時候。——柏拉圖

名句故事

　　The light here means truth. If men are afraid of truth, they prefer to stay in the darkness, which means that they live in ignorance or self-denial. It is a real tragedy. No one will blame a child for being afraid of the dark since a child is a child.

The child's fear of the dark gradually decreases with age. After becoming an adult, he or she usually won't choose to stay in the darkness even if no longer afraid of the dark.

Staying in the darkness is metaphorically living in ignorance. Only by exposing oneself to the light can one know truth.

這裡的光明是指真理。如果人們害怕真理，就比較喜歡待在黑暗之中，這意味著他們活在無知或自我否定之中。真的很悲哀。沒人會因小孩害怕黑怕而加以責備，因為小孩就是小孩。

小孩對黑暗的恐懼會隨著年紀逐漸降低。在成年之後，他或她通常不會選擇待在黑暗裡，即便已不再害怕黑暗。

待在黑暗之中在比喻上就是活在無知之中，只有讓自己曝露在陽光之中才能明白真理。

句型文法解析

配合本單元要介紹的文法概念，我們可以把哲學名句改寫為：It is easy for us to forgive a child who is afraid of the dark. 其意思和原句差不多。

電影《窈窕淑女》（My Fair Lady）裡有一句經典台詞 "How kind of you to let me come"，意思是「您真好讓我來這裡」，句中用到這個單元要介紹的慣用法，即 **It is** +形容詞+**for / of**+人+**to V**，kind 這類形容詞後面要接 of，例如：It is kind of you to help me.（你真好，幫我。）

同類形容詞還有 nice、wise、good、clever、silly、wrong、foolish、stupid、careless、rude、polite。後面接 for 的形容詞有：safe、easy、hard、right、likely、useful、difficult、pleasant、important、necessary、interesting、impossible、dangerous。

例如：

It is necessary for us to work hand in hand.（我們一起努力是必需的。）

It is easy for us to make mistakes.（我們犯錯是很容易的。）

It is impossible for him to give up the plan.（要他放棄那個計劃是不可能的。）

　要活用這種句型，就得把涵蓋在內的兩類形容詞背下來，別無他法，不背就容易搞錯。後面接 of 的形容詞通常是在描述人的某種特質，像是 nice、wise、foolish。

　It is kind of you to help me. 可改為 You are kind to help me. 其他同類形容詞可依此類推。後面接 for 的形容詞通常是在描述某種狀況，而不是人的特質。所以 It is impossible for him to give up the plan. 不能改成 He is impossible to give up the plan.

英文例句

接著就來看看 it is...(for / of +sb.)+to V 可以怎樣應用到句子中吧！

✡ **It is foolish of you to think** that one can be healthy and happy all the time.
你愚蠢地以為人可以一直保持健康快樂。

✡ **It is important for us to develop** good reading habits from an early age since such habits will influence us for our whole life.
很早就培養良好的閱讀習慣對我們來說很重要，因為這類習慣會影響我們一輩子。

✡ **It is kind of you to let me know** that you will seriously consider my proposal for fun outdoor activities.
你真好讓我知道你會認真地考慮我的趣味戶外活動提案。

4 ▶ Wh- do you think+S+V

哲學名句

Only the dead have seen the end of war. ——*Plato*

只有死人才見過戰爭的結束。——柏拉圖

名句故事

The quote might be interpreted as an irony. It means that war won't come to an end until all people are dead.

When people live, they fight with each other for land or money. Their personal conflicts might turn into a war if more people are involved. As long as they are alive, it is not easy for them to end a war once it gets started. They will kill each other until one side surrenders. It is usually how a war is ended.

But when a war is over, another war is looming on the horizon. In the history of mankind, there does not seem to have been a long-lasting peace anywhere in the world.

這句引言或許可解釋為一種反諷。意思是戰爭要到所有人死後才會結束。

當人們活著時，會為土地或金錢相互爭奪。如果參與的人數越多，個人之間的衝突就演變為一場戰爭。只要他們還活著，就不太容易在戰爭啟動之後停止戰爭。他們會相互廝殺直到其中一方投降為止。戰爭通常是這樣結束。

不過當一場戰爭結束時，另一場戰爭又在醞釀當中。在人類的歷史裡，世界各地似乎不曾有過持續長久的和平。

句型文法解析

某甲說：Who do you think has seen the end of war?（你認為誰見過戰爭的結束？）某乙回答：Only the dead.（只有死人），這樣的問答其實就是在說 Only the dead have seen the end of war.

常聽人說，Who do think you are?，意思是「你以為你是誰？」對方當然知道你是誰，只是不知道你知不知道你自己是誰。所以這句話的目的是在表達一種貶抑，不能傻傻的回答，Of course, I know who I am. 這樣扯下去就會很白目。

這個句子引導出本單元要介紹的句型，即**疑問詞+do you think+S+V?** 例如：Who do you think she is? 此時的意思就不是在貶抑，而是在問別人是否知道她是誰。

What do you think has happened?（你認為發生了什麼事？）

Where do you think she lives?（你想她住哪裡？）

Whom you think the characters in the movie represent?（你認為電影裡的角色代表的是誰？）。

這類句型所用到的動詞當然不只 think，還有 imagine、suppose、believe、fancy、consider、say、regard、guess 等。

記得 do+you+think 後面要接直述句，不能說成 Who do you think are you? 一定要說 Who do you think you are?

其實就是一種間接問句的概念：Do you know who she is? 是正確的說法，Do you know who is she?則是錯的。

接著就來看看 Wh- do you think+S+V 可以怎樣應用到句子中吧！

✡ **What do you think** he means when he says he still needs some time to think about our proposal?
你認為當他說還需要一點時間來考慮的我們的提案時是什麼意思？

✡ **Whom do you think** the teacher is talking about as she says someone should pay more attention to school work?
你認為老師說某人應該更注意一下學校課業時是在說誰？

✡ **Where do you think** we will be if we can live to be 100 years old and still capable of remembering things?
你認為如果我們能活到一百歲且記憶力還管用，人會在哪裡？

5 ▶ It is / was... that...

🏛 哲學名句

Courage is knowing what not to fear. ——*Plato*

勇氣就是知道不該害怕的是什麼。——柏拉圖

📖 名句故事

We all know what courage is, but we are not so sure about fear.

We are afraid of many things, such as snakes, darkness, spiders, and blood. But being afraid of these things does not mean that we do not have courage. It is just human nature to fear these things.

Why are we afraid of them? What we fear is the fear inside ourselves. If we can recognize it, we will become less afraid of the things mentioned above. We might even be able to overcome the fear. We will know by then what courage means.

We do not need to be physically strong to have courage. Courage is more about mental strength.

我們都知道什麼是勇氣，卻對恐懼不是那麼確定。

我們害怕許多的事物，譬如蛇、黑暗、蜘蛛及血。但害怕這些事物並不表示我們沒有勇氣，對它們感到害怕乃人之常情。

我們為何會怕它們？我們怕的是我們內在的恐懼。如果能認清這一點，就會對前述的事物比較沒那麼害怕，甚至能克服恐懼，到時就知道勇氣的意義為何。

我們不需要體格強壯才能擁有勇氣，勇氣和心靈的力量比較有關係。

句型文法**解析**

按照本單元要介紹的文法概念，哲學名句 Courage is knowing what not to fear. 可以說成 It is courage that makes one know what not to fear. 或是 A man of courage knows what not to fear. 前一個句子用到本單於要介紹的 **It is...that** 句型。

常聽到有人說，It is you that are to blame. 意思是你是應該受到責難的人，說成 You are to blame. 亦可，It is...that 句型就是把需要強調的人或事物放到前面，**it is 或其過去式 it was 永遠都是單數，功能就是把這個句型帶出來。**

例如：
It was John that bought a birthday present for Mary.
It was Mary that John bought a birthday present for.
這兩個句子裡的 that，第一個可以用主格的關係代名詞 who 代替，第二個則可以用受格的關係代名詞 whom 代替。

It was in the park that John met Mary yesterday.
It was yesterday that John met Mary in the park.
這兩個句子一個強調的是地點，另一個則強調時間，前者可用 where 代替 that，後者可用 when 代替 that。

記住 that 句子裡的動詞單複數型態完全由 that 之前所要強調的詞語來決定。

例如：It is you that are to blame. 是正確的說法。
It is you that is to blame. 則為不正確。

另外，這種句型也能強調從屬子句，例如：It is because the weather is good that we feel happy.

英文例句

接著就來看看 it is / was... that...可以怎樣應用到句子中吧！

✡ **It is the president of the country that** has the responsibility to create a better life for the people and ensure the security of the country.
國家的總統有責任為人民創造更好的生活並確保國家的安全。

✡ **It is because the students study hard that** their teachers are happy for them and plan to give them gifts of encouragement.
因為這些學生用功讀書，他們的老師為他們感到高興並計畫送他們禮物做為鼓勵。

✡ **It was at the train station that** Peter met by chance an old friend whom he had not seen for many years.
彼得在火車站碰到一位多年沒見的老朋友。

6 It is / has been + 一段時間 + since

哲學名句

The direction in which education starts a man will determine his future in life. ——Plato

一個人的教育起始方向將決定他未來的生命。——柏拉圖

名句故事

Education can change a man's life. What's especially important is the direction in which education starts a man.

If the first lesson we learn in school is about how to respect elderly people, we are most likely to keep that attitude toward older people for the rest of our lives.

If the first lesson is about how to make money, we might want to become businessmen in the future.

Without education, we will not be able to learn things in a systemic way. The teacher who initiates a student into one direction or another will influence the student for the rest of his / her life.

教育能改變一個人的生命。教育的起始方向尤其重要。

如果我們在學時的第一門課是如何尊敬年長者，我們很可能在接下來的生命裡保持這種對待年長者的態度。

如果我們所學的第一門課是如何賺錢，以後可能就想要成為商人。

沒了教育，我們將無法有系統地學習東西。將學生帶往某個方向的啟蒙老師，將會影響學生的一輩子。

句型文法解析

　　要把這個單元的句型套用在哲學名句上有點困難，但還是可以試試：It has been a long time since people last talked about the direction of education for a student and its influence on his / her future.（已經很久沒人討論學生的教育方向及其對學生未來的影響）。

　　碰到很久沒見的人時，我們通常會說，**It has been a long time since I last saw you.** 當然現在很多人都用 Long time no see. 這種中式英文來表達，主要是因為簡潔有力。

　　本單元介紹 **It is / It has been+一段時間+since** 這個句型，很常用的，不難，可是有時候還是會搞錯。例如：It has been ten years since we last saw each other. 這個句子前面用完成式後面用簡單過去式，從屬子句幾乎都是用簡單過去式，前面的主要字句有時用完成式有時用簡單現在式，意思各不相同。

　　It is already three years since he was a teacher. 句子的意思不是他當了老師三年了，而是他三年前還是老師（用簡單過去式表達過去的狀態），不當老師後已經三年了，意思大不相同。

　　把 since 字句擺在句子的前半部也可以，例如：Since I was at this company, they have had two managers. 句子的意思是我離開公司後換了兩位經理，since 子句用簡單過去表示過去式的一種狀態，不是持續的狀態，如果動詞用的表示持續狀態的動詞（如

work、live、stay），就表示狀態是從過去延續到現在。

英文**例句**

接著就來看看 it is / has been + 一段時間+since 可以怎樣應用到句子中吧！

✡ **It has been quite a long time** since we last saw each other and had a drink together at a bar in downtown Taipei.
自從我們上次在台北市中心一家酒吧碰面喝酒已過了很長一段時間。

✡ **It is five years** since Paul was a teacher, so he needs to make some preparation if he wants to teach again.
保羅不當老師已有五年，所以如果他想要重拾教職，需要做一點準備。

✡ **Since** you left the company, we **have experienced** a lot of change, including pay cuts and heavier workloads.
自從你離開公司後，我們經歷了許多變化，包括減薪和工作量增加。

1 It is said

📖 哲學名句

At his best, man is the noblest of all animals; separated from law and justice he is the worst. ——Aristotle

人類在最好的狀態下是所有動物中最高貴的；一旦脫離了法律和正義，人類卻是最糟的。——亞里斯多德

📖 名句故事

At their best, humans are the most intelligent species on earth and the noblest of all animals. But they can be the worst of all creatures if they deviate from law and justice.

Criminals are an example. They are people who commit crimes. They do not respect law and justice. They do whatever they want. They might be intelligent, but their intelligence does not help them become good members of society.

Society needs law and justice to function properly; otherwise, the world will be in a state of chaos. Humans at their best are people who are capable of being a model to others.

　人類在最好的狀態時是地球上最聰明的物種及最高貴的動物，但一旦脫離了法律和正義，人類卻可能是最糟的一種動物。

　罪犯就是一種例子，他們是犯罪之人，不尊重法律和正義。他們或許很聰明，但他們的聰明才智卻無法幫他們成為社會的善良份子。

　社會需要法律和正義才能正常運作，否則整個世界將陷入混亂之中。處於最好狀態的人是能夠成為他人模範的人。

句型文法解析

隨著時代演進，人類是不是最高貴的動物開始有了不同的答案，因此哲學名句可以改成 Man is believed to be the noblest of all animals. 或是 It is believed that man is the noblest of all animals.

使用 be believed to 這個句型就在表示只是相信所說的事物，沒有說它不是永恆不變的真理。

我們經常用到「**據說…**」這個句型，英文也有相對等的句型：**It is said+that** 子句，said 的位置可以用 **believed**、**reported**、**estimated** 這幾個過去分詞來代替，但意思就不太一樣，it is believed 是據信，it is reported 是據報導，it is estimated 是據估計，但同樣後面都是接 that 所引導的名詞子句。

例如：It is said that a typhoon is coming. 把句子改成 A typhoon is said to be coming. 亦可。

It is said that he made an mistake. 由於 that 子句是用過去式，改成以人為主詞的句型時必須在 be said to 後面接完成式，即 He is said to have made a mistake. 這樣的句型轉換原則也套用在 believed、reported、estimated 這幾個過去分詞上。

當我們說 It is believed that health is above wealth. 時，意思就是 Health is believed to be above wealth.

而 It is reported that five people were injured in the car accident. 則等於 Five people are reported to have been injured in the car accident.

另外，It is estimated that the meeting will last four hours. 則相當於 The meeting is estimated to last four hours.

這種句型變換不難，要特別注意的是前後時態不同時，轉換成以人或物為主詞的句型時就要用到完成式。

英文例句

接著就來看看 It is said 可以怎樣應用到句子中吧！

✡ **It is said that** women live longer than men, but not many people know the reason why.
據說女人活得比男人久，但知道原因的人不多。

✡ **It is said that** the police plan to give tickets to car drivers who illegally park their cars in downtown areas during rush hours.
據說警察打算對尖峰時間在市中心區違規停車的駕駛開罰單。

✡ **It is said that** there is life on Mars, but no evidence has been found so far as to the possibility.
據說火星上有生命，但到目前為止都還沒有找到可支持這種可能性的證據。

2 ▶ They say that

🏛 哲學名句

Pleasure in the job puts perfection in the work.

——Aristotle

樂在工作才有完美的表現。——亞里斯多德

📖 名句故事

If you enjoy doing your job, you tend to become more interested in what you are doing. You are also more willing to work a little longer.

The much effort you put into your job will make it more possible for you to do a better job, if not to get it done perfectly.

People love to say that the devil is in the details. That's certainly true.

But if you do not like your job, it is very hard for you to pay attention to the details. The result is that you will never attain perfection in your job.

如果你喜歡你的工作，你通常會對你所做的事情比較感興趣，也比較願意多花一點時間。

你付出的許多努力會讓你比較有可能把工作做好，如果不是把工作做到完美的話。

人們喜歡說魔鬼藏在細節裡，的確是這樣。

但如果你不喜歡你的工作，就很難讓你專注一些細節，結果你永遠無法在工作上達到完美。

句型文法解析

按照本單元所要介紹的句型，哲學名句可以改寫成：People say that pleasure in the job puts perfection in the work.（人們都説樂在工作才有完美的表現）。

上個單元介紹了 It is said that 句型，其實意義相同的類似句型還有 **They say that**、**People say that**、**Someone says that**，這個句型簡單很多，只要在 that 子句中加入你想要表達的東西即可，在句型轉換上可以和 It is said that 相互轉換。

例如：They say that he is an actor. 可轉換成 It is said that he is an actor. 或 He is said to be an actor.

另外兩個 People say that 和 Someone says that 也是同樣的用法。用 People say that 時可以有一點變化，像是 Some people say that，意思是某些人説，people 泛指一般人，People say that 就是指一般人都這麼説，可是換成 Some people say that 時，就代表部分人的説法或看法。

前一個單元提到，和 It is said that 相類似的句型還有 It is believed that、It is reported that、It is estimated that，可是除了 believe 外，report 和 estimated 都沒有衍生出類似 They say that 和 People say that 的句型。

所以有 They believe that 和 People believe that 句型，可是卻沒聽過 They report that 和 People report that 句型或是 They estimate that 和 People estimate 句型。

這些字詞的意思和功能雖然類似，但不見得能完全相互套用。

英文例句

接著就來看看可以怎樣應用這類的句型吧！

✡ **They say that** girls usually score higher marks in exams than boys, but that's not necessarily the case.
據說女生的考試成績通常比男生高，但不見得是這樣。

✡ **They say that** Peter failed in science exams, but he does not seem to be bothered about his poor performance in the exams.
據說彼得沒有通過科學測驗，可是他似乎沒有因考試成績不佳而受到影響。

✡ **People say that** the best way to live a happy life is to develop positive thinking, but I think that eating a healthy diet is more important.
據說過快樂生活的最佳方式就是發展正向的思考，可是我認為吃得健康更重要。

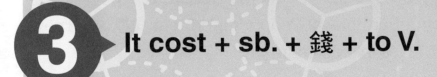

3 It cost + sb. + 錢 + to V.

 哲學名句

Love is composed of a single soul inhabiting two bodies.

——Aristotle

愛是由同時存在於兩個身體裡的單一靈魂所組成。

——亞里斯多德

名句**故事**

When a man and a woman fall in love with each other, they become a pair of lovers. They are each other's soul mates. You can say that they have a single soul dwelling in two different bodies. It is a feeling of wholeness that surfaces only when the soul-mate is found.

A soul-mate is defined as "a person with whom you have an immediate connection the moment you meet." It is similar to love at first sight.

But a single soul inhabiting two bodies means something more. It is not just love at first sight. You should have the feeling of wholeness as long as you are with your soul-mate.

當一個男人和一個女人彼此相愛時,他們成為一對情人,彼此的靈魂伴侶,你可以說他們擁有一個同時存在於兩人身體裡的靈魂。那是一種只有在找到靈魂伴侶時才會浮現的一體感覺。

靈魂伴侶在定義上是「你在一碰見時就立即產生連結的人」,類似一見鍾情。

但存在於兩個身體裡的單一靈魂具有更大的含義,不是一見鍾情而已。只要和靈魂伴侶在一起,你就應該有那種一體的感覺。

句型文法解析

根據哲學名句可衍生出愛情要兩人才行這個概念：It takes two people to make a relationship. 一個人叫做單相思，不在這裡加以介紹，而三人行就更不能公開討論。

當我們說花費多少金錢或時間買某樣東西或做某件事情時，經常用到的動詞有四個：**cost**、**pay**、**spend**、**take**。前面兩個都表示花錢，spend 用來表示花費時間或金錢皆可，take 主要是指花費時間。

本單元先介紹 cost，其基本句型是：物品+cost(s)+金錢：It + cost(s) + 人 + 金錢 + to verb。

例如：
The comic book cost NT$200.
The comic book cost me NT$200.
It cost me NT$200 to buy the comic book.
這三個句子都對，表達的是同一件事情，即自己花了新台幣 200 元買下一本漫畫書，由於買的動作已經發生，所以時態用過去式。

這個句子也可以說成 I paid NT$200 for the book. 或 I spent NT$200 on the comic book.

英文的特色之一就是可以用許多不同句型或同義字來表達同樣的概念，所以學習起來有點難度。如果你還沒買下某樣物品，只是想知

道需要花費多錢，賣家在用 It cost(s)句型時就會採取未來式：It will cost you about NT$500,000 to buy a car.

英文例句

接著就來看看可以怎樣應用這類的句型吧！

✡ **It costs the parents a lot of money to have** their children study at a private school, but they think it is worth the money.

這對父母花了許多錢讓自己的小孩唸私立學校，可是他們認為錢花得值得。

✡ How much do you think <u>it will cost you to buy</u> a three-bedroom apartment in downtown Taipei?

你認為在台北市中心買一個三房公寓要花多少錢？

✡ **It will cost you nothing to dream**, and everything not to. You do not have to spend any money making a dream, but if you do not dream, you will miss a lot.

做夢不會花你任何的錢，不做夢卻會讓你花上所有的一切。做一個夢不必花上一毛錢，可是如果連夢都不做，你將失去很多。

4 sb. spend + 錢 + (in) V.ing / on + sth.

 哲學名句

We are what we repeatedly do. Excellence, then, is not an act, but a habit. ——*Aristotle*

我們是反覆的行為所累積而成。所以卓越不是一種行為，而是一種習慣。——亞里斯多德

名句故事

Many people say that we are what we eat. It is certainly true. We are also what we do.

If you want to be excellent at something, you must do it repeatedly until you are completely familiar with it. For example: the best way for a man to be good at a sport is to keep on practicing. As the saying goes, practice makes perfect.

People love to attribute excellence to intelligence. As a matter of fact, excellence is just a habit.

Everyone has the ability to excel at something, but the problem is that not many people have the patience to do the same thing again and again.

許多人說我們吃什麼就變成什麼，確實是這樣。我們也是我們所做的事累積而成。

如果你想要在某樣事情上表現卓越，就必須反覆做那件事情直到完全熟悉為止。例如：對某項運動產生專精的最佳方式是反覆練習。如俗諺所說：熟能生巧。

人們喜歡把卓越歸因於聰明才智，事實上，卓越只是一種習慣。

每個人都有能力專精某樣事情，可是問題是，有耐心反覆做同一件事情的人並不多。

句型文法解析

　　配合本單元要介紹的句型，可以將哲學名句改為：Excellence is nothing but a habit that takes a long time to develop.（卓越只是一種需要長時間培養的習慣）。

　　本單元專門介紹 **It + takes + 人 + 時間 + to V** 這個句型，意思某人花了多少時間做某件事情，這是最常用的句型，也可以用另外兩個替換句型：**人 + take(s) + 時間 + to V** 或 **V-ing + takes + 人 + 時間**。

　　例句 It took Paul three hours to do the job.
　　Paul took three hours to do the job.
　　Doing the job took Paul three hours.
　　這三個句子都對，只是不同的句型轉換，考試最常考這種。

　　要注意的是，take 只表示花了多少時間，不會用來表示金錢，表達花了多錢買某樣物品時要用上一單元介紹的 It + cost(s) + 人 + 金錢 + to V 句型。

　　It + takes + 人 + 時間 + to V 句型的問句形式為：How long did it take Paul to do the job?或 How long did Paul take to do the job?也可用 spend 來表示花費的多少時間，例如：Paul spent three hours doing the job.

　　不過通常表達花了多時間時還是以 take 為主，因為這樣比較不會

搞混，表達時間時用 take 就好，表達金錢就以 cost 和 spend 為主。

另外，take 也可以用來表達花了多少努力，例如：It took me a lot of effort to do the job.

接著就來看看可以怎樣應用這類的句型吧！

✡ **It took me two days to write** a report that my English teacher assigned to me.
我花了兩天時間才寫好英文老師所指定的報告。

✡ How long do you think **it will take to get a master's degree** in English Literature?
你認為拿到英國文學碩士學位要多久時間？

✡ The new president of the country says that he will do whatever **it takes to defend his country**, a statement showing his determination to strengthen the military's combat capabilities.
國家的新任總統說他將盡其所能來保衛他的國家，此番聲明顯示他強化軍隊戰鬥力的決心。

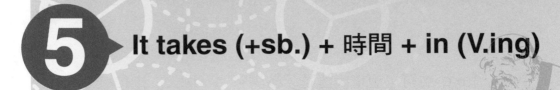

5 It takes (+sb.) + 時間 + in (V.ing)

🏛 哲學名句

In all things of nature there is something of the marvelous.

——Aristotle

自然的萬物皆有奇妙之處。——亞里斯多德

📖 名句故事

What this quote means is that even the smallest insect is marvelous because its structure involves a lot of unsolved mysteries. To solve these mysteries, some people become scientists. Some scientists are especially interested in insects and animals. They are categorized as "biologists."

Philosophy is the source of many different fields of study today. It allows people to be curious about all things of nature. Such curiosity leads to the development of different fields of study, such as biology and astronomy.

It is a sense of wonder that all children have as they start exploring the world. Scholars need to keep this sense of wonder to make further studies.

這句引言的意思是，即使最小的昆蟲也很奇妙，因為牠的身體結構牽涉到許多未解之謎。為了解開這些謎團，有些人成了科學家。某些科學家對昆蟲和動物特別有興趣，他們被歸類為「生物學家」。

哲學是現在許多不同學門的源頭，它讓人對自然萬物產生好奇之心。這樣的好奇心引導了生物學和天文學等學門的發展。

那是一種所有孩童在開始探索世界時都有的驚奇之感，學者要保持這種驚奇之感才能在研究上有所精進。

句型文法解析

根據哲學名句，我們可以衍生出這樣的句子：In all things of nature that we spend time on, we can find something of the marvelous.（在我們花時間觀察的自然之物中，我們都可以發現奇妙之處）。

這個單元專門介紹 spend，之前提過它既可以表示花了多少錢，也可以表示花了多少時間，和主要表達時間的 take 及表達金錢的 cost 很不一樣。它也沒有以 it 虛主詞開頭的句型，都要以人為主詞。

例如：He spent most of his pocket money on books.（他把大部分的零用錢用在買書上）。這是標準的說法，也可以說 He spend most of his pocket money for books. 通常是以 on 為主，比較少人用 for。

另外，人 + spend + 金錢或時間 + in + V-ing 也是一種常用的句型，介系詞 in 通常可以省略，例如：He spent most of his spare time (in) reading novels.（他把大部分的空閒時間用在讀小說上）。

但要注意的是，也有 spend time to do something 這個說法，但意義不同於 spend time doing something，前者表示要花多少時間來做某件事，後者的意思是花了多少時間來做某事，一個是還沒有做，另一個則是已經做了，不過大部分狀況還是要用 spend time doing something，所以不用過於擔心。

英文例句

接著就來看看可以怎樣應用這類的句型吧！

※ If you want to save money, you need to **spend as little as possible on** luxury items, such as gold watch and diamond.
如果你想要省錢，就盡量少花錢在金錶和鑽石之類奢侈品上。

※ A man who **spends very little time on** himself often cannot stand the feeling of loneliness.
一個很少花時間在自己身上的人，通常無法忍受孤獨之感。

※ In order to expand the business of our company, we must **spend more money buying** new equipment and recruiting enough employees.
為了擴展我們公司的業務，我們必須花更多的錢在購買新設備和招募足夠的員工上。

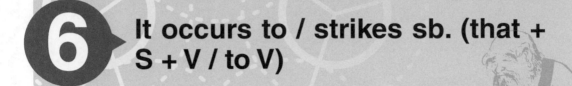

6 It occurs to / strikes sb. (that + S + V / to V)

哲學名句

Knowing yourself is the beginning of all wisdom.

——Aristotle

認識自己是所有智慧的開端。——亞里斯多德

名句故事

Not many people know themselves. They do not know it until the painful moment of self-awakening arrives. At that moment, they will be forced to know themselves in a painful way. But they will become wiser afterwards. Aristotle is right in saying, "Knowing yourself is the beginning of all wisdom."

Many people love to criticize others without recognizing the fact that they might be the subject of criticism as well.

Once we start consciously examining our faults and weaknesses, we can view ourselves from someone else's eyes. It is the moment of self-awakening. It will not be a pleasant experience, but we will get through it one way or another.

認識自己的人並不多。他們毫不自知直到痛苦的自我覺醒的那一刻來臨,到時,他們將被迫用一種痛苦的方式認識自己,但之後會變得比較有智慧。亞里斯多德説得真對:「認識自己是所有智慧的開端」。

許多人喜歡批評他人,卻無法認清自己可能也是被批評對象這一事實。

一旦我們開始有意識地檢視我們的錯誤和弱點,就能用其他人的眼光來審視自己,那是自我覺醒的一刻,雖然不會是一種愉快的經驗,我們總有辦法度過。

句型文法解析

　　根據本單元要介紹的句型，可以把哲學名句改為：It strikes me as a universal truth that self-knowledge is the beginning of all wisdom.（在我看來，自我認識是所有智慧的開端，這是一個普遍的真理）。

　　好幾個社群網站上都有類似這樣的句子：It occurs to me that for each and every one of you on my friends list, I catch myself looking at your selfie pictures as well as sharing jokes and news that I think might be interesting to you.（我突然想到，對我好友名單上的每一位朋友，我發現我都在看你們的自拍照片，也分享我認為你們會感興趣的笑話和新聞）。

　　這個句子用到 **It occurs to+人+that** 子句句型，意思是某人突然想起某件事情，某件事情可以 **that** 子句或不定詞片語來表達。類似意義的句型還有 It strikes + 人 + as + adj. + that 子句。

　　例如：It strikes me as odd that the man never speaks to me every time we meet.（我突然覺得每次碰到那人時他都沒有跟我說話很奇怪）。

　　比較常用的是 It occurs to+人這個句型，裡面的 that 子句也可以用不定詞片語代替。

例如：

It suddenly occurred to her that she forgot to do an important thing.（她突然想到忘了做一件重要的事情）

It didn't occur to her to ask how the accident happened.（她沒有想到要問意外是怎麼發生的）。

英文例句

接著就來看看可以怎樣應用這類的句型吧！

✵ **It occurs to me that** I don't have to get up early today since summer vacation has started.

我突然想到今天不用早起，因為暑假已經開始了。

✵ **It struck him as odd that** she didn't accept the job offer, but he was confident that she would change her mind.

他對她沒有接受工作邀約感到奇怪，但他相信她會改變心意。

✵ **It didn't occur to her to make** a phone call to the restaurant to confirm her reservation for a table for two.

她沒有想到打電話給餐廳確認所訂的兩人座位子。

2 西方哲思：

我思故我在

1 ▶ S believe / find ...

哲學名句

I think; therefore I am. ——Rene Descartes

我思故我在。——笛卡兒

名句故事

Rene Descartes, who was a 17th century French philosopher, is considered to be the father of modern Western philosophy because he created a whole new system of thought that helped shape modern philosophy. "I think; therefore I am" is his most famous quote.

Descartes argues that a man knows his existence through thinking. Our sense of perception can be deceptive. A candle that we are watching might not really exist. It could be something that we reconstruct in our imagination.

In this way, we can doubt the certainty of everything. But the very fact that we are doubting shows that we do exist.

17 世紀法國哲學家笛卡兒被認為是現代西方哲學之父，因為他創造出一套新的思考系統，協助形塑了現代哲學。「我思故我在」是他最有名的引言。

笛卡兒辯說，人經由思考知道自己的存在。我們的感官知覺會騙人。我們看到的蠟燭或許不是真實存在，可能是我們想像力重新塑造之物。

經由這種方式，我們可以懷疑每一種事物的真確性。但我們在懷疑這一事實卻顯示我們的存在。

句型文法解析

　　笛卡兒這句名言現在有許多不同的搞笑版本，像是：I eat, there I am.（我吃故我在）或 I sleep, therefore I am.（我睡故我在），不管是哪種版本，都和本單元介紹的文法概念沒關。真正有關的句子是：I believe it necessary to think because thinking makes us feel connected with the world.（我相信思考有其必要，因為思考讓我們感到與世界的連結）。

　　有人說"I find it hard to believe that we are in heaven."，意思是我很難相信我們是在天堂，這個句子用到 **find + it + adj. / N. + to V** 句型，**believe**、**consider**、**think** 等動詞也可套用到這個句型。

　　例如：
I found it interesting to talk with an elderly man.（我發現和年長者聊天很有意思）

We believe it necessary to fight for what we believe in.（我們相信有必要為我們相信的東西而戰）

I consider it strange to wear a hat inside a building.（我認為在室內戴帽子很奇怪）。

　　這種句型還可以複雜一點，例如：I find it necessary for him to take a rest.（我覺得有必要讓他休息一下）；I find it necessary to take rest.（我發現有必要休息）這個句子是指我需要休息，前一個句子是說他需要休息，多了一個 for him 就意思完全不同。

　　另外，這個句型裡的受詞補語也可以用名詞，例如：We find it nonsense to say that everyone is a good person.（我們發現每個人都是好人這個說法沒有意義）。不過名詞作為受詞補語的機率不大，還是以形容詞居多。

英文例句

接著就來看看可以怎樣應用這類的句型吧！

❈ Whether you believe it or not, **you will find it boring to have** too much leisure time.
不管你相不相信，你將發現休閒時間太長反而很無聊。

❈ **The teacher believes it necessary for students to behave** in a proper way. But his students might think otherwise.
老師相信有必要要求學生保持恰當的行為，可是學生或許不這麼想。

❈ Some scientists **think it possible for humans to live** to 200 years old in the future, but there is no knowing how they will look like at that age.
某些科學家認為人類有可能活到 200 歲，但無人能知他們到了那個年紀會有怎樣一個容貌。

2 ▶ take N. for granted

〽 哲學名句

The reading of all good books is like a conversation with the finest minds of past centuries. ——*Rene Descartes*

閱讀好書就像是與過去許多世紀最優秀的心靈交談一樣。

——笛卡兒

📖 名句故事

A book is an expression of the author. It tells a lot about the author. We can know through the text what kind of person the author is. What's more important, we learn something from the values of life that the author puts into the book.

Reading the book is like having a conversation with its creator, who beats his or her brains out to write something moving the reader.

What we can learn from the conversation depends on how much we like the book and whether we understand its nuanced meaning. It is a two-way communication. As we make more response to the book, it will also give us more feedback.

書是作者的表達，透露許多與作者有關的東西。我們可以經由文章知道作者是怎樣一個人，更重要的是，我們學習到作者在書中所表達的生命價值。

閱讀書就像是與創作者對話，他或她可是絞盡腦汁才寫出感動讀者的東西。

我們能從這樣的對話學習到什麼，要取決於我們有多麼喜愛那本書及我們是否了解書中的微言大義，這是一個雙向溝通，當我們對書有更多的反應時，書也會給我們更多的回饋。

句型文法解析

　　根據本單元要介紹的句型，哲學名句可以改寫為：Although reading good books is like conversing with the greatest minds of the past, don't take it for granted that they will answer to your requests.（雖然閱讀好書就像是與過去最偉大的心靈對談，但不要認為他們一定會回應你的要求）。

　　我們常聽到有人說**不要把某件事情當成理所當然**，英文的相對應說法就是，**Don't take it for granted.** 這是一種說法，另一種句型是 **take it for granted that** 子句，這裡的 it 是虛受詞，用來代替後面 that 所引導的名詞子句，前一個句子裡的 it 則具體地指某樣事物。

　　例如：
Don't take friends' help for granted.（不要把朋友的幫忙視為理所當然）

　　Mary takes it for granted that her boyfriend will give her whatever she wants.（瑪麗認為男友給她任何她想要的東西是理所當然的事情）。

　　當某人說，Don't take my help for granted. 意思是不要把我的幫助視為理所當然，可是 Don't take it for granted that I will help you. 卻不太一樣，意思是不要以為我一定會幫你，但目前還沒幫上任何的忙，只是對方一廂情願地認為一定會得到協助，前一個句子表

示已經幫了忙，說話者要聽者不要把這樣的幫忙當成理所當然。

　有人說，Don't take your life for granted，意思是不要把你活著當成理所當然，聽起來有點在嚇人。

英文**例句**

接著就來看看可以怎樣應用這類的句型吧！

✡ Most workers in Taiwan **take overtime for granted**, but it might not be so in more advanced countries, such as Britain and France.

台灣大多數勞工都把加班視為理所當然，但在英國和法國這些比較先進的國家或許不是這樣子。

✡ Government officials **take it for granted** that the new regulations will be implemented as scheduled. They don't consider the possibility that some people might boycott the regulations.

政府官員把如期實施新規定視為理所當然，他們沒有考慮有人杯葛的可能性。

✡ Some parents love to tell their children not to **take their money for granted**.

一些父母喜歡跟小孩說，不要把他們的錢視為理所當然。

3 ▶ that... this...

哲學名句

When it is not in our power to determine what is true, we ought to follow what is most probable. ——*Rene Descartes*

當我們的能力不足以決定什麼是真實的時，

就應該遵循什麼是最有可能的。 ——笛卡兒

名句故事

Sometimes we may not be able to find a true answer. We have no choice but to accept the most possible answer.

For example, if you want to buy a car, you don't necessarily know what is the best choice for you. You don't need to find out the answer, since it might take too much time. Just take your pick.

It is always difficult to make a decision because once a decision is made, it might be impossible to undo it.

We all face tough decisions at one time or another. Make the decision according to the most possible options at hand.

我們有時或許無法找到真正的答案，只能接受最可能的答案。

例如：如果你想買一部車子，你不見得知道什麼是你的最好選擇。你不需找出答案，因為可能會花上太多時間。選你喜歡的就好。

下決定總是很困難，因為一旦做了決定，就可能無法改變。

我們都會在生命的某些時刻碰上困難的抉擇，要根據手上最可能的選項做出決定。

句型文法解析

按照哲學名句，我們可以做這樣的改寫：What is true might be more important than what is most probable, but this is more easily accessible than that.（真實的東西或許比最有可能的東西還要重要，但後者卻比前者更容易取得）。

有一種句型看似簡單，卻很容易犯錯。舉例來說，當我們說，Health is more important than wealth, for this cannot give us as much happiness as that.（健康比財富重要，因為財富不能像健康那樣給予我們那麼多的快樂）。

句子裡 this 指的是後者，也就是財富，而 that 則是前者，代表健康，這樣的句型相當於 the former...the latter（下個單元再介紹）。

要記住，**this 是指後者，that** 則指前者，很容易搞錯。再來一個例子：Work and recreation are both important; this gives us energy to work and that gives us money to play.（工作和休閒都很重要；休閒讓我們有能量工作，工作則讓我們有錢玩樂）。

這種句型碰上複數名詞時，則用 **these** 和 **those** 來代替 this 和 that，不過出現的機率並不高，主要還是以 that...this 為主。

例如：Dogs are closer to humans than cats; these are more independent, and those like to play with humans.（狗比貓更

親近人類；貓比較獨立，狗則喜歡和人類玩耍）。

英文例句

接著就來看看可以怎樣應用這類的句型吧！

✵ Father and mother are both important; **this gives you** a lot of love, and **that gives you** other kinds of support.

父親和母親都很重要；母親給你很多的愛，父親則給你其他的支持。

✵ Eating well and eating healthy are different things; **this is meant to** make you become healthier, and **that is mainly for purpose of** satisfying your desire for good food.

吃得好和吃得健康是不同事情；吃得健康是要讓你變得更健康，吃得好則主要是要滿足你對美食的渴望。

✵ Effectiveness is not the same as efficiency; **this is primarily about** using the least amount of time and energy to do a job, and **that means** doing the job in a successful way regardless of the time and energy spent.

有效力不同於有效率；有效率主要是指用最少的時間和精力來做一件工作，有效力則是用成功的方式完成工作，不論所花的時間和精力。

4 ▶ the former... the latter...

ⅢⅢ 哲學名句

An optimist may see a light where there is none, but why must the pessimist always run to blow it out?

——Rene Descartes

樂觀者可以在沒有光的地方看到光，但悲觀者為何一定要過去把光滅掉？——笛卡兒

名句故事

The quote tells the difference an optimist and a pessimist. An optimist always looks on the bright side, while a pessimist tends to think negatively. A pessimist is a man who thinks all men are bad, but an optimist is one who thinks they are good.

If a pessimist and an optimist see a doughnut at the same time, the former sees the hole and the latter the doughnut. Why not be an optimist?

An optimistic individual can see the light of possibility in things, showing a way out for people around him. Our society needs such a person to give us a ray of hope in hard times.

這句引言說明樂觀者和悲觀者之間的差別。樂觀者總是往光明面看，悲觀者則傾向於負面思考。悲觀者認為所有人都是壞的，樂觀者則認為所有人都是好的。

如果悲觀者和樂觀者同時看到一個甜甜圈，悲觀者看到的是甜甜圈中間的洞，樂觀者看到的是甜甜圈。那何不當個樂觀者？

一個樂觀的人能夠在事物中看到可能的光芒，為周遭的人引導一個出路。我們的社會需要這樣的人來為艱困年代的我們帶來希望的光芒。

句型文法解析

哲學名句可以衍生這樣的句子：An optimist sees a light where there is none, while a pessimist tries to blow out the light. The former inspires hope, while the latter attempts to destroy any kind of hope.（樂觀者在沒有光的地方看到光，而悲觀者則嘗試滅掉那個光。前者引發希望，而後者則試圖摧毀任何一種希望）。

上個單元介紹 that...this 句型，這個單元就換意思相同的 **the former...the latter** 句型，兩個句型可以相互替換。

例如：
Henry and Peter are good friends; the former is a police officer, and the latter is a college professor.（亨利和彼得是好朋友；亨利是警官，彼得是大學教授。）

Man differs from animals in that the former can speak, while the latter can't.（人類不同於動物之處是在於人類能夠說話，動物不能。）

也可以用 the one...the other 句型來表示和 the former...the latter 同樣的意思，還有人用 the first...the second，但比較少見。

例如：To study or to play? I prefer the latter option to the former.（是要讀書還是玩樂？我比較喜歡後一個選項。）

Diligence and intelligence are both necessary for a man to succeed ; the first is sometimes more important than the second.（勤奮工作和聰明才智都是成功所必要的；前者有時比後者還要重要。）。

英文例句

接著就來看看可以怎樣應用這類的句型吧！

✡Grammatical accuracy and rich vocabulary are important elements in writing; **the former** shapes the structure, **and the latter** provides the content.

文法正確和字彙豐富是寫作的重要元素：前者形成結構，後者提供內容。

✡She is having a difficult time choosing between two great universities, Harvard and Yale; **the former** is more attractive to her **but the latter** offers her a scholarship.

她在哈佛和耶魯這兩間名校之間做一抉擇時碰到難題；哈佛對她比較有吸引力，可是耶魯卻要給她獎學金。

✡He likes to eat apples and bananas; **the former** helps him keep the doctor away, **and the latter** gives him a lot of energy.

他喜歡吃蘋果和香蕉；蘋果幫他遠離醫生，香蕉給他許多能量。

5 ▶ It appears / seems that...

Whenever anyone has offended me, I try to raise my soul so high that the offense cannot reach it. —Rene Descartes

一旦有人冒犯了我，我就試著把我的靈魂提高到一個冒犯不到的層次。—笛卡兒

名句故事

We all meet rude people once in a while. We are likely to be affected by their offensive words or behaviors. We may want to treat them in the same way, which means our self-control and moral standards have been dragged down as a result.

On an occasion like this, you have to raise your soul to a

level where you are immune to negative influences.

You don't need to get angry. Just stay calm and keep your consciousness in a state where you feel peaceful. Learn how to deal with rude people in a wise way. You'll become a better man in the process.

我們偶而碰到粗魯的人，可能會受到他們冒犯性言詞或行為的影響。我們或許會想用同樣的方式對待他們，這意味著我們的自我控制和道德水準都因而被往下拉。

碰到這樣的情況，你必須把自己的靈魂提高到一個不會受到負面因素影響的層次。

你不必生氣，只要保持冷靜並把自己的意識保持在平和的境界。學習如何用明智的方式對待粗魯的人，你會在過程中變得更好。

句型文法解析

　　順著本單元要介紹的句型，哲學名句可以改成這樣：Whenever anyone has offended me, I do not seem to be angry since I try to raise my soul so high that the offense cannot reach it. （一旦有人冒犯我，我似乎沒在生氣，因為我試著把我的靈魂提高到一個別人冒犯不到的層次）。

　　我們常見到 **It seems / appears +that** 子句這個句型，算是最常用的句型之一，所以一定得熟悉才行。這種句型可以改為**以人為主詞，+ seem(s) / appear(s) + to V** 的結構。

例如：
It seems that he is a good man.
等於 He seems to be a good man. （他似乎是個好人。）

It seems that Mr. Wang was rich when he was young.
等於 Mr. Wang seems to have been rich when he was young. （王先生似乎在年輕時曾經有錢過。）

It appears that the storm is coming.
等於 The storm appears to be coming. （暴風雨似乎要來了。）

It seemed that he was angry.
等於 He seemed to be angry. （他似乎生氣了。）

　　從這些例句可以看出，句型的轉換都按照一定的模式，比較複雜的是時態的變化：當前面是現在式，that 子句裡是過去式時，改用以人為主詞的說法就要用到不定詞的完成式，如 Mr. Wang seems to have been rich when he was young. 如果前後都是過去式，以人為主詞的句型就用過去式，但如果 that 子句用到過去完成式，就要這樣改：It seemed that he had made a mistake. 改成 He seemed to have made a mistake.（他似乎犯了一個錯誤。）

英文例句

接著就來看看可以怎樣應用這類的句型吧！

✡ **It seems that** the man who I met on the street yesterday is a crime suspect the police are looking for.
我昨天在街上碰到的那個人似乎是警察正在尋找的犯罪嫌疑犯。

✡ **It appears that** some of the big companies are in trouble because of the collapse of the stock market.
某些大公司似乎因股市崩盤而有了麻煩。

✡ **It seems that** he missed the chance to make a big fortune by selling his house to a real estate agent at a very high price.
他沒有把房子高價賣給房屋仲介，似乎錯過了發大財的機會。

6 ▶ It (so) chances / happens that...

川 哲學名句

The greatest minds are capable of the greatest vices as well as of the greatest virtues. ——René Descartes

最偉大的心靈既能為最大之惡，也能為最大之善。——笛卡兒

名句故事

We all know what a virtue is. For example, humility is a virtue. But we may not be sure about what a vice is. It is not equal to an evil. A vice is defined as "a moral fault or weakness in someone's character." Greed, pride, and envy are considered to be vices.

A virtuous man might be greedy and proud at the same time, but he won't let these vices overpower his mind. It is like a struggle between good and evil, but not quite.

We are just ordinary people. We admit that we have weaknesses and vices. We need time to conquer these weaknesses to become better persons.

我們都知道美德是什麼。例如,謙遜是一種美德。但我們可能不確定什麼是惡。它不等同於罪惡。惡被定義為「性格中的道德缺陷或弱點」。貪婪、驕傲、及嫉妒皆被視為惡。

善良的人可能同時具有貪婪和驕傲這兩種惡質,但不會讓這些惡質掌控他的心靈。就像是善與惡之間的鬥爭,但並不完全如此。

我們只是平凡之人。我們承認我們有弱點和惡質。我們需要時間來克服這些弱點,成為更好的人。

句型文法解析

根據哲學名句,我們可以衍伸出這樣的句子:It just happens that the greatest men do the best deeds.(偉大的人只是碰巧做了最善良的事。)

當我們說碰巧怎樣時,英文的相對應說法為 **It (so) chances / happens that + S + V** 或人**+chance(s) / happen(s)+to V**。

第一個句型是以 it 為虛主詞，第二個句型則以人為主詞，

例如：It happens that Tom meets her. / Tom happens to meet her. （湯姆碰巧遇到她）

Peter chanced to meet his boos. / It chanced that Peter met his boss.（彼得碰巧遇到他的老闆）

It seemed that he was unable to do the job. / He didn't seem to be able to do the job.（他似乎無法做這份工作）。

從這些例句可以了解這兩種句型的互換方式，還有否定時的用法。另外，疑問句時要這麼說：Did Peter chance to meet his boss?

如果覺得 It happens / chances that 這個句型麻煩，不妨多用以人為主詞的句型，比較不會出錯。譬如，如果你剛好來到台北，請讓我請你吃一餐這句話翻成英文，就只能採用以人為主詞的句型：If you happen to be in Taipei, please let me treat you to dinner.

有個類似的句型不要搞混了，sth happens to someone 是某人發生了某事的意思，例如：I don't know what has happened to him.（我不知他怎麼了）。

英文例句

接著就來看看可以怎樣應用這類的句型吧！

✡ **It happened that** I was taking a shower as the phone rang. So I missed the phone call from a person, who I later found out to be a very important client.

電話鈴響時我剛好在沖澡，所以錯過了電話，後來才發現是一位重要客戶打來的。

✡ **It happens that** Tom knows the answer to that question. The teacher praises him for his good performance. Tom may not be the best student. He just happens to know the answer.

湯姆剛好知道問題的答案，老師誇獎他的好表現。湯姆或許不是最好的學生，只是剛好知道答案。

✡ **It happened that** two old men were walking slowly across the street as a car ran the red light. They were hit by the car as a result.

一輛車闖紅燈時剛好有兩位老人在緩慢地過馬路，結果撞到了他們。

7 one... another... / one... the other... / some... others...

哲學名句

Common sense is the most widely shared commodity in the world, for every man is convinced that he is well supplied with it. ——*René Descartes*

常識是世界上最廣泛分享的商品，因為每個人都深信自己擁有充分的常識。——笛卡兒

名句故事

If you are in a public place, don't show your money and valuables. This is an example of common sense. Even a child knows it.

But it is often the case that many people, regardless of age, like to show off their wealth in public, such as wearing diamond watches and jewelry.

Their behavior violates common sense. They do not lack common sense, however. It is their vanity that makes them deviate from common sense. Common sense is the most widely shared commodity in the world. It is so easily available that people tend to ignore or forget about it.

如果在公共場合，不要顯露自己的金錢和貴重物品。這是一種常識，連小孩都知道。

但不分年紀，許多人經常喜歡在公共場合炫耀自己的財富，像是露出手上的鑽表和身上戴的珠寶。

他們的行為違反了常識。但他們並不缺常識，是虛榮心使他們偏離了常識。常識是世界上最廣泛分享的商品，由於隨手可得，以致於容易被忽略或忘記。

句型文法解析

　　每個人都深信自己擁有充分的常識，事實上並不見得如此。因此根據哲學名句，我們可以衍伸這樣的句子：We have two options. One is to have common sense, and the other is to pretend that we do.（我們有兩個選項，一個是擁有常識，另一個是假裝我們有。）

　　英文裡的 another 和 other 意思很接近，常常有人搞錯，尤其是考試時。簡單來說，用 **another** 來表示另一個時，所指涉的事物至少有三個；而 **the other** 則是指兩個中的另一個。搞懂這個基本原理後，才好介紹 one... another... / one... the other... 這兩組句型。

　　例如：

Mr. Wang has two brothers; one lives in Taipei and the other in Taichung.（王先生有兩個兄弟，一個住在台北，另一個在台中）

Mr. Wang has three brothers; one is a teacher, another a doctor, and the other a police officer.（王先生有三個兄弟，一個是老師，一個是醫生，另一個是警官）。

　　one... the other 句型比較容易理解，但提到三個時，第一個要用 one，第二個用 another，第三個才用 the other，因為提到第一個時是三選一，所以用 one，提到第二個時還有兩個選項，所以用

another，提到第三個時只剩一個選項，只能用 the other。

當你説我不喜歡這個東西，給我另一個時，可以用 another 或 the other，用 another 表示有三種以上的選項，如果用 the other，就表示只剩一種選項。

英文例句

接著就來看看可以怎樣應用這類的句型吧！

✡ We have two options. **One** is to do nothing, and **the other** is to try the best we can.

我們有兩個選項，一個是什麼也不做，另一個是盡力而為。

✡ Henry has three favorite hobbies. **One** is reading novels, **another** is playing basketball, and **the other** is listening to music. He has enough common sense to know that he can do these hobbies only in his free time.

✡ 亨利有三個最喜歡的嗜好，一個是閱讀小説，一個是打籃球，另一個是聽音樂。他有足夠的常識知道，只能在空閒時間從事這些嗜好。

✡ To say is **one thing**, and to do is **another thing**. In other words, actions speak louder than words. Don't judge a person's ability only by what he or she says.

説是一回事，做則是另一回事。換句話説，事實勝於雄辯。不要只根據某人的言語來評斷其能力。

1 cannot / may / must

🏛 哲學名句

If a man will begin with certainties, he shall end in doubts; but if he will be content to begin with doubts, he shall end in certainties. ——*Francis Bacon*

如果以肯定作為出發點，最終將以疑問作結，然如果願意以疑問作為出發點，最終將以肯定作結。——培根

📖 名句故事

This quote is applicable especially to a scholar. If the scholar feels sure of the subject that he is researching, he will gradually find that it is not as easy as he originally thought. It is better to begin with doubts, which will lead the scholar to find out the answer.

Begin a research with an open mind, and you will learn more in the process. The more you learn, the more you are unsure of your knowledge.

Francis Bacon, a 17th century English philosopher, is considered to be the father of scientific method because of his insistence on the use of a skeptical and methodical approach.

這句話特別適用於學者。一位對所研究主題很有把握的學者，會逐漸發現不是如他原先所想的那般容易。最好從疑問出發，這樣才能引導學者找出答案。

以開闊的心胸來起始一項研究，就會在過程中學到更多。學得越多，就會對自己的知識越感到不確定。

英國 17 世紀哲學家培根被認為是科學方法之父，因為他堅持採用懷疑論及方法論。

句型文法**解析**

根據哲學名句，我們可以衍伸出這樣的句子：If a man begins with doubts, he may end in certainties.（如果能夠以疑問作為出發點，最後可能會以肯定作結。）

英文最常用的助動詞有 can、may、must，搞清楚這三個的用法，就足以應付大部分的情況。這些助動詞的基本句型如下：

肯定句是主詞+ can、may、must + 原形動詞

否定句是主詞+ can、may、must + not + 原形動詞

疑問句是 Can、May、Must + 主詞 + 原形動詞？

can 表示能力、可能、允許，過去式為 **could**。

may 表示請求、許可、可能。

must 表示必須、應該、一定，過去式為 **had to**。

例如：

You may watch TV, but you must do your homework first.（你可以看電視，但必須先做功課）

She can run faster than I.（她能跑得比我還快）

May I use your phone?（我能借你的電話用一下嗎？）

也可以用 can 來表示請求，但 may 比較正式且常用；I may go out tomorrow.（我明天或許會外出）

也可以用 might 來代替 may，但此時的 might 不是 may 的過去式，而是表示可能性比 may 還低；You must get up early.（你必須早起）意思就等於祈使句的 Get up early.

英文例句

接著就來看看可以怎樣應用這類的句型吧！

✧ Student A: "**May** I go to the bathroom?" Teacher: "Yes, you may." Student B: "**Can** I go to the bathroom?" Teacher: "You can, but you may not. Ask in a correct way."

A 學生：「我可以去洗手間嗎？」老師：「是的，你可以去」。學生 B：「我能夠去洗手間嗎？」老師：「你能夠去，可是不可以去。要用對的方式來問才行」。

✧ What are the things that you **must** do in Taipei? Going to a night market may come to your mind first. But if you begin with certainty, you might end up feeling disappointed.

在台北一定要做哪些事情？你首先想到的可能是去夜市。但如果你以肯定作為出發點，最後的結果可能感到失望。

✧ Jane **can** do the job better than Mary, but her salary is not as much as Mary's. Fortunately, Jane is content to begin with a modest salary so that she **can** end in higher incomes.

珍能把工作做得比瑪莉好，可是她的薪水卻沒有瑪莉多。幸好珍對普通的起薪感到滿足，這樣最後才能得到較高的收入。

2 should / ought to have p.p

哲學名句

Money is a great servant but a bad master.

——*Francis Bacon*

錢是很棒的僕人，卻是很糟的主子。——培根

名句故事

Everyone loves money, but not everyone knows how to control money without being controlled by it.

If you have money, it will serve you in a pleasant way. But if you have too much money, you will be enslaved by it.

Or if you owe money to some people, you will live in constant fear of being asked to pay back the debt.

We cannot go a day without money in modern life. But money is not everything. We must keep it under our control. We should not live for money. We should earn money in an honest way.

每個人都喜歡錢，但不是每個人都知道如何控制錢且又不會被錢控制。

如果你有錢，它會把你伺候得高高興興。但如果你有了太多錢，你會被錢所奴役。

或者如果你欠某人錢，你將經常活在被討債的恐懼之中。

現代生活不能一天沒有錢，但錢不是所有的一切。我們必須控制好錢，不應該為了錢而活。我們應該用誠實的方式賺錢。

句型文法解析

根據哲學名句，我們可以衍伸這樣的句子：We should have had money be a great servant.（我們本應該讓錢當個好僕人。）

助動詞 **should** 後面接 **have+**過去分詞有兩種意思，一是表示對過去的確認，意即「應該做了…」，另一是對未做的事表示責難和後悔，意思是「該做而未做」。should 可以換成 ought to，意思和用法一樣。

例如：

The game should / ought to have started in the morning.（這場比賽應該已經在早上開始了）意思是確認比賽已經展開。

You should have taken some rest.（你應該休息一下）意思是你該休息卻沒有休息。

We should not / ought not to have bought that car.（我們不該買下那部車。）否定時把 not 放在 should 和 ought 之後即可。

看完這些意思和結構比較複雜的句子後，He should not buy that car. 這個句子或許會讓你猶豫一下，其實不要想太多，意思很簡單，就是不該買那部車，不管是現在還是未來。

另外，You should drink more water. 和 You should have drunk more water. 這兩個句子都對，前者是説你目前和未來都該

多喝一點水，後者是說你本該多喝一點水，可是你沒有。

英文例句

接著就來看看可以怎樣應用這類句型吧！

✴ Mr. Lin **should have been** more careful when he posted a negative comment on his Facebook page. His comment got many likes. Public recognition is a good servant but a bad master. It can turn you into a different person.

林先生在他的臉書頁面上張貼一則負面的評論時應該要更小心一點，他的評論引來許多人按讚。公眾的認同是很棒的僕人，卻是很糟的主子，會把你變成不同的人。

✴ The young couple **should not have spent** most of their money buying a new house, since they do not have much money left and have to borrow money from friends.

這對年輕夫婦不應該把大部分的錢用在買新房子上，因為他們只剩下一點點錢，必須向朋友借錢過日子。

✴ The government **should have taken** better care of the homeless, who live on the street like stray dogs.

政府應該給遊民更好的照顧，這些遊民像流浪狗一樣住在街上。

3 ▶ be used to

哲學名句

Knowledge is power. ——Francis Bacon

知識就是力量。——培根

名句故事

"Knowledge is power" is one of the most popular maxims in the world. It is as famous as other proverbs like "Honesty is the best policy" and "The early bird catches the worm."

But not many people know it was said by 17th century philosopher Bacon. What it means is that knowledge is more powerful than physical strength and that the more knowledge a person has, the more powerful he is.

The Chinese proverb "A book holds a house of gold" tells

about something similar. But you had better not take it for granted that your knowledge will make you become richer.

「知識就是力量」是世界上最受歡迎的格言之一，歡迎程度相當於「誠實為上策」和「早起的鳥兒有蟲吃」等諺語。

但很少人知道它是出自 17 世紀哲學家培根之口，意思是知識比身體的力量更為強大，知識越多，就越強大。

中國諺語「書中自有黃金屋」表達出類似的意思。但最好不要認定知識一定會帶來更多的財富。

句型文法解析

根據哲學名句，我們可以衍伸這樣的句子：People are used to pursuing power through knowledge.（人們習慣透過知識追求力量。）

慣用語 **be used to** 是習慣於的意思，**這裡的 to 是介系詞，所以後面要接動名詞**，不是原形動詞。be accustomed to 的意思和用法相同。

例如：

I am used to the noise.（我習慣了噪音。）

I am used to driving in Taipei.（我習慣了在台北開車。）

It was a long time before she was completely used to working with them.（過了很長一段時間她才完全習慣與他們一起共事）可以在 used 之前加上副詞來形容。

I am quite used to the new rules.（我很習慣新的規定。）

You'll get used to living in the country.（你會逐漸習慣鄉間的生活。）用 get 代替 be 是為了表達逐漸形成的意思，grow used to 和 become used to 也有同樣的意思。

Little by little, Tom became used to his new friends.（湯姆

逐漸習慣他的新朋友。）

I am not used to eating American food.（我不習慣吃美國食物。）否定句時只要在 used 之前加上 not 即可。

另外，不要看到 be used to 就以為是在表示習慣，例如：Wood is used to make paper. 意思不是木材習慣於造紙，而是木材被用來造紙。看到句子時還是要先想一下，不要做直覺性反應。

英文例句

接著就來看看可以怎樣應用這類的句型吧！

✧I **am used to** getting up early. This is a habit that I have developed since childhood.

我習慣早起，這是一個從兒童時期培養起的習慣。

✧If you **get used to** the new environment, you will find that it is not as bad as you thought.

如果你習慣了新的環境，你將發現不是你想的那麼糟。

✧After having tried spicy food several times, I **am now used to** it and kind of like it. It is not that spicy, after all. Habits are powerful as knowledge is power.

試過幾次辛辣食物後，我現在已經習慣且有點喜歡上那種味道，畢竟沒那麼辣。習慣的力量強大有如知識為力量。

4 used to

ⅠⅠⅠ 哲學名句

It is impossible to love and be wise. ——*Francis Bacon*

不可能在陷入愛情的同時，又能保有智慧。——培根

名句故事

When a man loves a woman, he finds that there is no place for wisdom in love. Love is passion, while wisdom is devoid of passion. How can the two opposite things mingle together?

Many people say that love is without reason. You can analyze love in a scientific way because love is a complex chemical reaction.

But love is more than a chemical reaction. It involves a

mysterious feeling which is beyond the reach of science. When you fall in love with someone, you experience one of the most beautiful moments in your life. Such experience is so wonderful that any scientific explanation will only ruin it.

男人在愛上女人時會發現戀愛過程中沒有智慧存在的空間。愛就是激情,而智慧則缺乏激情。這兩種相反的東西如何能混在一起?

許多人說愛是沒有理智。可以用科學的方法來分析愛,因為愛是一種複雜的化學反應。

然愛不只是一種化學反應,所牽涉到的神秘感覺是超越科學所能解釋的範圍。陷入愛河時,會經驗到生命中最美妙的時刻。這樣的經驗是如此之好,以致於任何的科學解釋都會破壞它。

句型文法解析

根據哲學名句,我們可以衍伸這樣的句子:Some people used to consider themselves wise until they fell in love. (有些人曾經認為自己很有智慧,直到他們談了戀愛。)

和 be used to 看起來有點類似的是 **used to**,但**表示過去的習慣**,不是現在的習慣。

例如：

I used to smoke.（我過去常抽煙。）

The old building used to be a movie theater.（那棟老建築過去是電影院。）

I used not to like classical music.（我以前不喜歡古典音樂。）

否定句時把 not 加到 used 之後即可，但現在越來越多人用 didn't use to；Used you to play baseball?（你以前打棒球嗎？）疑問句時把 used 擺到句首即可，但現在也有人說，Did you use to play baseball?

要注意的是，used to 表示過去的習慣，現在已經沒這個習慣，當你說你曾在紐約住過三年時，只要用簡單過去式來表達即可：I lived in New York for three years. 不要說成 I used to live in New York for three years.

另外，always 之類頻率副詞也可以套用在 used 的前面或後面，例如：I always used to be afraid of big dogs.（我以前總是怕大狗。）

用 I used always to be afraid of big dogs. 亦可。

used to 搭配 there is 句型的用法：There used to be an

illegal structure in the park.（公園裡以前有個違章建築。）

🌾 英文例句

接著就來看看可以怎樣應用這類句型吧！

✧ Peter **used to be** rich, but he spent away all of his money in a few years. He now lives in debt. It is impossible to be rich and wise at the same time.

彼得曾經富有，可是幾年內就把錢花光。他現在舉債度日。不可能同時既有錢又有智慧。

✧ Helen **used to be** the most beautiful girl in school, but she is now so fat that only her old friends can recognize her. It is impossible to be fat and beautiful at the same time.

海倫曾經是學校裡最美麗的女孩，可是她現在胖到只有老朋友才認得。不可能同時既胖又美麗。

✧ There was a time when Tom was the leader of the class. Tom **used to be** the class leader.

湯姆在某段期間是班上的班長，他曾經是班長。

5 ▶ may well + V / may as well + V

哲學名句

Age appears best in four things: old wood to burn, old wine to drink, old friends to trust and old authors to read.

——*Francis Bacon*

四種東西越老越好：老木材好燒，老酒好喝，老朋友好信任，老作家好讀。——培根

名句故事

Old wines are like old friends, since they are the best as they mature with years. But they need to be good when they are young. Old wood burns well as compared to green wood which is too damp to burn. Old authors refer to old books, which are classics in literature such as Shakespeare's plays and Jane Austen's novels.

Old books can be read again and again, while new books do not have the same value. We remember famous scenes in a literary classic because they are created in a beautiful way.

We should appreciate old things. Do not treat them as something disposable.

老酒就像是老朋友，因為陳年的酒最好，但酒在年輕時也要品質好才行。老木材比較好燒，青嫩的木材則太潮濕不好燒。老作家指的是老書，也就是文學經典名著，像是莎士比亞的戲劇和珍・奧斯汀的小說。

老書可一讀再讀，而新書則沒有這樣的價值。我們所以會記得經典文學作品中的著名場景，是因為這些場景是以美妙的方式創造出來。

我們應該欣賞老東西，不要把它們當成可丟棄的東西。

句型文法解析

根據哲學名句，我們可以衍伸出這樣的句子：Ages may well appears best in four things: old wood to burn, old wine to drink, old friends to trust and old authors to read.（四種東西理應是越老越好：好木材好燒，老酒好喝，老朋友好信任，老作家好讀。）

有些慣用語看起來很類似，中間只差一個字，可是意思卻差很多，may well+V 和 may as well+就是一個例子，**前者的意思是理應、難怪、大可，後者是最好和不妨的意思，相當於 had better，但語氣比較委婉。**

例如：

You may well be tired after the trip.（你在這趟旅行後理應累了。）

She may well be angry with him.（她理應對他發脾氣。）

Capable of doing many things, he may well be called a talented man.（能做許多事的他，當然稱得上是一個有才能的人。）

You may as well keep your promise.（你最好維持你的承諾。）

You may as well take care of yourself.（你最好照顧好你自己。

You don't have that much money. You might as well stop

thinking about buying a car.（你沒有那麼多的錢，你最好別再想要買部車。）

也可以用 might as well，意思比 may as well 委婉一點。注意 may as well 和 had better 之間的差別：We may as well eat something. 和 We had better eat something（我們最好吃點東西。）看起來一模一樣，可是前者意思是沒有其他事情可做，不如吃點東西，後者是我們應該吃點東西。

英文例句

接著就來看看可以怎樣應用這類句型吧！

✡ She **may well want to go to** the movies with you. Don't miss the chance. This is an advice from an old friend.
她可能想和你去看電影，別錯過了機會。這是老朋友的忠告。

✡ The new novel **may well become** a best-seller because it has a very interesting story.
這本新小書很可能成為一本暢銷書，因為它的故事內容很有趣。

1 獨立不定詞片語

川 哲學名句

It is not a lack of love, but a lack of friendship that makes unhappy marriages. ——Friedrich Nietzsche

婚姻不快樂不是因為缺少愛，而是因為缺少友情。——尼采

名句故事

What does the quote mean? Does it mean that friends are more important than love in a marriage? Actually, what it means is that a pair of lovers need to be friends first before they can enter into a relationship. If they do not form enough friendship, they will not be able to build a happy marriage. They stay with each other just to keep their marriage despite the fact that they do not live happily together.

What kind of friendship does a marriage need? Not many people know the answer. Perhaps the answer lies in the famous proverb "A friend in need is a friend indeed."

這句引言的意義為何？意思是朋友比愛情對婚姻更為重要？事實上，意思就是一對戀人要先成為朋友才能進入愛情關係。如果沒有足夠的友情，他們將無法建立快樂的婚姻關係，這樣生活在一起只是為了保持婚姻關係，儘管過得並不快樂。

婚姻需要哪種友情？知道答案的人不多。或許答案就在「患難之交才是真正的朋友。」這句諺語中。

句型文法解析

根據哲學名句，我們可以衍伸出這樣的句子：To cut a long story short, love and friendship make happy marriage.（簡言之，婚姻快樂要有愛和友情。）

說到獨立不定詞片語，不見得每個人馬上就知道是什麼，可是如果一提 to tell the truth（老實說）和 to cut a long story short（簡言之）這兩個常見的詞語，大家馬上就耳熟能詳，它們就是獨立不定詞片語。

舉例來說，**to be brief**（簡言之）、**to sum up**（總之）、**to**

make the matter worse（更糟的是）、**to return to the subject**（言歸正傳）、**to begin with / start with**（首先）、**to say nothing of**（更不用說）、**not to speak of**（更不用說）、**not to mention**（更不用說）等都是一些很常見的獨立不定詞片語。

　　這些片語是副詞片語，修飾全句之用，可置於句首、句中及句尾，有轉折語氣的功能。

　　例如：

To tell the truth, I really don't know who that man is.（老實說，我真的不知道那個人是誰。）

Tom didn't like the new rule. To make the matter worse, he broke the rule on purpose.（湯姆不喜歡新的規定，更糟的是，他還故意不遵守新的規定。）

This house is very ugly, to say nothing of its being small.（這棟房子很醜，更不用說又小。）

To sum up, teachers should encourage their students to do more outside reading.（總之，老師應該鼓勵學生多閱讀課外讀物。）

接著就來看看可以怎樣應用這類句型吧！

✡ **To tell the truth**, your failure to submit papers on time has angered your teacher. You might not get a good grade. It is your lack of punctuality, not your lack of intelligence, that makes the teacher become angry.

說實話，你未能準時交報告已經惹怒了老師，你可能不會得到好成績。不是因為你缺乏聰明，而是因為你不遵守交報告時間，老師才會生氣。

✡ **To begin with**, you should get everything prepared for the dinner party on the weekend. Don't screw it up. It is your attitude that matters most in the process.

首先，你應該把週末晚餐聚會所需的東西準備好，別搞砸了。重要的是你在過程中展現的態度。

✡ **To cut a long story short**, Bill passed the final exam not because he studied hard but because he was just lucky enough. It was pure luck, not diligent study, that made Bill pass the exam.

長話短說，比爾通過期末考不是因為用功讀書而是因為運氣好。純粹是運氣，而不是用功讀書，比爾才得以通過考試。

2 ▶ had better / best + V

〣〣 哲學名句

That which does not kill us makes us stronger.

——Friedrich Nietzsche

沒有弄死我們的將使我們更堅強。——尼采

名句故事

We all have to confront something difficult in our lives. If we can live through it, we will become stronger. We might make some mistakes in the process of overcoming that difficulty. As long as we learn from those mistakes, we will be able to deal with the same or a similar situation in the future. That's how we become stronger and wiser.

No matter how many mistakes you make, you will make it to the end if you keep on trying. You will see the light at the end of the tunnel. Nothing is more precious than that moment.

　我們在一生當中都會碰上困難之事，如果能夠安然度過，就會變得更堅強。我們在克服這些困難時或許會犯一些錯誤。只要我們從錯誤中學習，以後碰到同樣或類似的狀況時就知道怎麼處理。那是我們變得更堅強和有智慧的緣故。

　不管犯了多少錯誤，只要持續嘗試，就會撐到最後。你將看到隧道口的光線，沒有什麼東西可以比那一刻更有價值。

句型文法解析

　根據哲學名句，我們可以衍伸出這樣的句子：We had better cherish challenges because that which does not kill us makes us strong.（我們最好珍惜挑戰，因為那殺不死我們的，使我們更強壯。）

　前面的單元有提過 had better（最好），用 had best 也可以，但還是以 had better 為主。使用這個詞語時要注意不要對年紀比自己大的人說 You had better... 這樣很不禮貌，通常是年紀大的人對年紀較輕的人說 You had better... 說起來很簡單，但一不注意還是會犯錯。所以 **had better** 基本上就是給人建議，**had** 通常和主詞縮寫在一起，像是 **you'd（you had）**、**I'd（I had）**、**we'd（we**

had）。

　　否定形式是在 had 後面加上 not，例如：You had better not break your promise.（你最好不要違背你的承諾）。

　　如果有附加問句，還是要用 had，例如：We'd better go, wouldn't we?這個句子是錯的，要改成 hadn't we?在疑問句也是把 had 擺在句首，例如：Hadn't we better tell him the truth?（我們不該告訴他實情嗎？）這裡的 hadn't we better 就是 we had better 的意思，有點弔詭，否定反而成了肯定。

　　在口語中，had 常常被省略。
例如：
You better go home now.（你現在最好回家）

You better try again.（你最好再試一次）。

　　had better 雖然是在給人做建議，事實上就是要對方照著做就對了，沒什麼好商量的。

英文例句

接著就來看看可以怎樣應用這類句型吧！

✡ We **had better** get the job done as soon as possible because the boss has said so. That which does not kill us makes us stronger.

我們最好盡快做好工作，因為老闆已經這麼說了。沒有弄死我們的將使我們更堅強。

✡ You **had better** keep your promise, or you will be considered to be a man who eats his words. That which ruins your reputation stays with you for the rest of your life.

你最好實踐你的承諾，不然你會被視為一個食言的人。毀壞你的名聲的將一輩子和你在一起。

✡ If you do not want to become the focus of attention, you **had better** not speak in such a loud voice. Everybody can hear what you are talking about. That which makes you famous also makes you fail.

如果你不想成為注意的焦點，最好不要這麼大聲說話，每個人都聽到你在說什麼。讓你成名的也會讓你失敗。

3 would rather... than...

川 哲學名句

I'm not upset that you lied to me, I'm upset that from now on I can't believe you. ——*Friedrich Nietzsche*

我不是因為你對我說謊而感到難過，

而是因為從現在起我將無法相信你。——尼采

名句故事

Lying itself is not that horrible. What is worse is that we can no longer trust the person who has lied to us.

Former U.S. President Bill Clinton lied about his sexual relationship with Monica Lewinsky, which caused the Democratic Party to lose in the 2000 U.S. presidential election. In 2015, a famous American journalist was found to have lied about his personal experience on a military plane hit by enemy fire during the U.S. invasion of Iraq in 2003.

In the same way, some people lie on their resume or make up outstanding records. It is human nature to lie, but the liar has to pay the consequences of losing other people's trust.

說謊本身並不是那麼可怕。更糟的是，我們無法再信任對我們說謊的人。

前美國總統克林頓對他和李文斯基之間的戀情撒了謊，導致民主黨輸了 2000 年總統大選。2015 年，一名知名美國記者被發現謊報 2003 年美國入侵伊拉克期間他在搭乘軍機時遭到敵火攻擊一事。

同樣的，有些人在履歷上作假或偽造傑出的紀錄。說謊是人類的天性，但說謊者必須付出失去他人信任的代價。

句型文法解析

根據哲學名句，我們可以衍伸出這樣的句子：I would rather accept the truth than the lie.（我寧願接受事實，也不要是謊言。）

慣用語 **would rather...than...** 是「寧願 A 而不是 B」的意思，

A 和 B 是對等的原形動詞，例如：I'd (would) rather stay at home than go out.（我寧願待在家裡而不是出去）would 經常和主詞縮寫在一起

A: How about a drink? B: I'd rather have something to eat.（A: 喝點東西如何？B: 我寧願吃點東西）
would rather 可單獨使用，不見得後面一定要接 than。

She would rather go to school than do nothing at home.
She would go to school rather than do nothing at home.
She prefers to go to school rather than do nothing at home.
She prefers going to school to doing nothing at home.

這四個句子都對，意思是「她寧願去學校，而不是待在家裡無所事事」，只不過是不同句型的轉換，would rather A than B 可以換成 would A rather than B、prefer to A rather than B、prefer A to B，下一個單元將專門介紹 prefer to 句型，就不在這裡多做說明。

另外值得一提的是，would rather 後面也可以接一個句子，有點像是 that 子句，不過不用把 that 寫出來，而且句子要用過去式，表示一種假設。

例如：
I'd rather you came now.（我寧願你現在來。）

My wife would rather we didn't see each other every day. （我的老婆寧願我們不要每天見面。）

英文例句

接著就來看看可以怎樣應用這類句型吧！

✡ She **would rather** stay at home **than** go out with you. You had better try harder. I am not upset that she declined to accept your invitation. I am upset that you did not work hard enough.

她寧願待在家裡而不是與你出去，你最好加把勁。我難過的不是她婉拒了你的邀約，而是你不夠努力。

✡ He **would rather** live his life in a happy way **than** watch himself wither away in sadness slowly. He thinks that there is no reason for sadness to last for a long time. He is upset that many people waste their time on sadness.

他寧願快樂地生活而不是看著自己在悲哀中逐漸萎縮，他認為沒有理由讓悲哀持續下去。他難過的是，許多人把時間浪費在悲哀上。

✡ I **would rather** you did not get involved in the matter. I was upset that you did not stick to your principles.

我寧願你沒有參與這件事情。我難過的是你沒有堅持你的原則。

4 ▶ prefer... to...

ⅢⅢ 哲學名句

Sometimes people don't want to hear the truth because they don't want their illusions destroyed.

——Friedrich Nietzsche

有時人們不想聽到真話，因為他們不想讓他們的幻想破滅。

——尼采

名句故事

Can we live without illusions? Some people live in illusions of one sort or another. It is like living in a dream. They do not want to wake up from the dream. If you destroy their illusions, they might not be able to live. What kind of illusions do they have? They might believe in a Utopian future, in which humans no longer have to worry about death. It is not a bad illusion, after all.

Some people live in ambitions that might never be fulfilled. They want to become rich, for instance. Not all of them can reach the goal. It is just a hope that gives them support in life.

沒有幻想我們活得下去嗎？有些人活在各種不同的幻想之中，像是活在夢裡。他們不想從夢裡醒來。如果你毀了他們的幻想，他們可能就活不下去。他們有著怎樣的幻想？他們或許相信一種烏托邦式未來，到時人類將不再擔心死亡。畢竟這樣的幻想並不壞。

有些人活在永遠無法實現的抱負之中。例如，他們想要變有錢。不是所有人都能達到目標，目標只是為他們的生命提供支撐的希望。

句型文法解析

這個單元介紹 prefer to，由於意思和用法在前一個單元有和 would rather...than 一起說明過，這裡就以實際的例子來進一步了解。例如：Sometimes people prefer not to hear the truth because they don't want their illusions destroyed.（有時候人們比較不喜歡聽真話，因為他們不想要讓他們的幻想破滅。）

這個句子是根據前面的哲學名句改寫而成，重點是運用到 prefer

to 的否定形式，也就是 prefer not to；如果用 would rather...than 的句型來改，則是：Sometimes people would rather not hear the truth than have their illusions destroyed.

回到 prefer to 這個句型上，我們要記得有三種變化，一是 **prefer A to B**、一是 **prefer A rather than B**、另一則是 **prefer to A rather than B**。

例句如下：
I prefer walking to riding.（我喜歡走路更甚於開車）

She prefers making cakes by herself rather than buying them in a shop.（她比較喜歡自己做蛋糕，而不是到店裡買）

I prefer to spend the weekend at home rather than go hiking in the country.（我寧願週末待在家裡，而不是到鄉間健行）。

同學們可能會對 prefer 後面什麼時候接動名詞，什麼時候接原形動詞感到困惑，其實不難，只要用 prefer to，後面一定接原形動詞，連帶 rather than 後面也是接原形動詞。

如果 prefer 後面沒有接 to，那就是 prefer A to B 句型，此時的 A 就是 prefer 的受詞，必須以名詞、代名詞、及動名詞的形式出現。

 **英文例句**

接著就來看看可以怎樣應用這類句型吧!

✡ Those who **prefer walking to driving** are often healthier because walking is a great way to improve or maintain health. This is an truth that some people do not want to hear.

喜歡走路甚於開車的人通常比較健康,因為走路是改善或維持健康的良好方式。這是某些人不想聽到的真相。

✡ Women **prefer to stay out of the sun** because they want to protect their skin and stay looking young. Sunshine is necessary for good health, however. Don't stay in the illusion that exposure to sunshine is bad for your skin.

婦女比較不喜歡接觸陽光,因為她們想要保護肌膚並維持年輕的樣貌,不過陽光卻是良好健康所必須的。不要停留在陽光有害皮膚這個假象之中。

✡ Jane **prefers to eat out rather than cook at home**, so she does not have to worry about how to clean the kitchen. She does not have to worry about hearing the truth about her cooking skills, either.

珍喜歡到外面用餐更甚於在家裡自己做菜,這樣就不用擔心要如何清理廚房。她也不用擔心聽到有關她的烹飪技巧的真實評語。

5 ▶ cannot (help / choose) but

 哲學名句

There are no facts, only interpretations.

——Friedrich Nietzsche

沒有事實，只有詮釋。——尼采

名句故事

This quote may not be as easy as it appears to be. The phenomena we observe through our senses are objectives facts. People tend to differ in their explanation of the meaning or significance of an objective fact. In other words, they have different interpretations of the same fact. It is like the interpretation of a book. There is no "correct" interpretation. Every interpretation has its own value. It represents a perspective.

The world becomes more meaningful because of the many different interpretations. Nietzsche also says, "You have your own way. I have my way. As for the right way, correct way and the only way, it does not exist."

這句引言可能不是如表面上看起來那麼簡單。我們經由感官觀察到的現象是客觀的事實。人們通常在解釋客觀事實的意義或重要性時會有所不同，換句話說，他們對同一事實有著不同的詮釋。就像是對一本書的詮釋，沒有「正確的」詮釋，每一種詮釋都有其價值，代表的是一種觀點。

世界因許多不同的詮釋而變得更有意義。尼采也說，「你有你的方式，我有我的方式。至於正確的方式、恰當的方式及唯一的方式，則完全不存在。」

句型文法解析

根據哲學名句，我們可以衍伸出這樣的句子：We can't help but look for the only fact.（我們都忍不住只尋求唯一的事實。）

慣用語 **can't help / can't choose but / can't help but** 都是「忍不住／無法不／不得不」的意思，其中只有 can't help 後面要接動名詞，其他兩個都是接原形動詞。

例如：I can't help laughing when I hear him sing.（我聽到他唱歌時忍不住笑了出來。）

也可以寫成 I can't help but laugh when I hear him sing.

或 I can't choose but laugh when I hear him sing.

I can't help liking her.（我忍不住喜歡上她）這個時候就要採用忍不住的意思，而不是不得不，所以不要以為句子簡單就掉以輕心，有時候反而會搞錯。

I couldn't help overhearing what they were talking about.（我忍不住偷聽到他們的談話內容）這個狀況有時候是忍不住有時候是不得不，如果你坐在咖啡廳，聽得到隔壁桌客人的談話內容，此時不聽也不行，一方面是人的好奇心，另一方面是無法脫離談話聲音的範圍。

I can't help thinking about her. 和 I can't help but think about her. 雖然是文法及意義上可以相互替換的句子，但兩者之間

還是略有不同，前者是我就是無法不想到她，意思她盤據在我的腦海裡，後者是我無法讓我自己不想她，程度上有點比不上前一個句子，當然這種細微的差異要到一定的英文程度才能體會出來。

英文例句

接著就來看看可以怎樣應用這類句型吧！

✡ The girl **couldn't help opening** the gift box to find out what was inside. There was a pretty doll in the box.

女孩忍不住打開禮盒來看看裡面有什麼，盒子裡有個漂亮的娃娃。

✡ The girl **couldn't help asking** everybody to do as she said. She ignored the fact that everybody had different ways of doing things.

她忍不住要大家都照她的步驟做，卻忽略了每個人的習慣不同。

✡ I **couldn't help but go** in the opposite direction because there was a traffic jam in the other direction.

我不得不走相反的方向，因為另一個方向發生了塞車。

1 too... to...

哲學名句

We are not rich by what we possess but by what we can do without. ——Immanuel Kant

我們不是因為擁有什麼而富有，而是因為能不擁有什麼。

——康德

名句故事

Many people complain about not earning enough money. They say that they have to pay a lot of bills each month. These bills include an electric bill, a phone bill, a water bill, and an Internet bill. They will be worse off if they have a housing loan and have to pay it back by monthly installments.

It is usually the case that they also buy a car on installments. They want to have too many things. Desires for material things should have limits. If your monthly salary is only around NT$25,000, there is just no reason for you to buy an iPhone.

許多人抱怨錢賺得不夠。他們說每個月要付一大堆帳單,這些帳單包括電費、電話費、水費、及網路通訊費,如果還有分期付款的房貸要繳,情況會更糟。這些人通常還會分期付款買車子。他們想要擁有太多的東西。物質的慾望應該有所節制。如果你的月薪只有 2 萬 5000 元左右,就沒有理由買一支 iPhone 手機。

句型文法解析

根據哲學名句,我們可衍伸出這樣的句子:It is never too late to realize that what we are rich not by what we possess but by what we can do without.(理解富有不在於擁有什麼,而在於能不擁有什麼,永遠不嫌晚。)

如諺語 "It is never too late to mend." 意思是「亡羊補牢,猶未晚矣」,句子用到 **too...to**(太…以致於不能)句型,也可以用 **so...that** 句型來表達:It is never so late that one cannot mend. 注意 that 句子要用否定形式。

我們可以按照"It is never too late to mend." 的模式造出類似的句子。

例如：It is never too late to learn.（學習永遠不嫌晚。）

It is never too late to fall in love.（談戀愛永遠不嫌晚。）

It is never too late to change careers.（換職業永遠也不嫌晚）

熟悉這個句型的最好方式就是多練習與 so...that 句型之間的轉換：

He is too young to go to school.（他太小，不能去上學。）
=He is so young that he can't go to school.

The news is too good to be true.（這消息好得不像是真的。）
=The news is so good that it can't be true.

如果在 too..to 之間加上 for someone，就更好改寫：
The food is too spicy for me to eat.（這食物辣到我不能吃。）
=The food is so spicy that I can't eat it.

The weather is too hot to work.（這天氣熱到我們無法工作。）
=The weather is so hot that we can't work.

The car is too expensive for him to buy.（這車貴到他無法買。）
=The car is so expensive that he can't buy it.

記住改成 so...that 句型後，that 句子裡的及物動詞後面要加上受詞，也就是 it。

英文例句

接著就來看看可以怎樣應用這類句型吧！

✵ It is never **<u>too late to</u>** learn. But you can't use it as an excuse for not learning at a young age.

學習永遠也不嫌晚，可是你不能拿來作為年輕時不學習的藉口。

✵ The hiker was **<u>too tired to</u>** go any longer. He took a rest at the roadside to regain his strength. He could go so far not by his strength but by his will.

健行者累到走不動，只好在路邊休息恢復體力。他能走這麼遠，不是靠著體力，而是毅力。

✵ Mr. Lin was **<u>too excited to</u>** speak as he won a lottery scratch-off game. He couldn't believe it at first. He originally planned to get rich not by luck but by hard work.

林先生在贏得刮刮樂彩金時興奮到說不出話來，他一開始還不相信。他原先打算藉著努力工作而不是運氣來變有錢。

2 ▶ can't... too...

🏛 哲學名句

He who is cruel to animals becomes hard also in his dealings with men. We can judge the heart of a man by his treatment of animals. ——*Immanuel Kant*

對動物殘忍的人在待人方面也會變得冷酷。我們可以根據一個人對待動物的方式來判斷他的內心。——康德

📖 名句故事

This quote takes on greater significance nowadays because there are more animal lovers than there were as Kant was alive. It seems that a philosopher, because of his love of wisdom, has love for all living creatures.

Long before Kant, ancient Greek philosopher and

mathematician Pythagoras had said, "As long as men massacre animals, they will kill each other. Indeed, he who sows the seeds of murder and pain cannot reap the joy of love." It is certainly true. But we may not be able to live without eating animal meat for the moment. What we can do is to treat our pets in a nice way.

　　這句引言現在更具有重要性，因為動物愛好者比康德在世時還要多。愛好智慧的哲學家似乎也愛所有的生物。

　　早在康德之前，古希臘哲學家暨數學家畢達哥拉斯就說，「只要人類持續屠殺動物，就會彼此相殘。的確，種下謀殺和痛苦種子的人，將無法獲得愛的愉悅。」確實是真的。但我們目前暫時無法不吃動物的肉，我們能做的就是善待自己的寵物。

句型文法解析

　　根據哲學名句，我們可以衍伸出這樣的句子：We can't be too careful to judge people. He who is cruel to animals is also hard on men.（分辨人時，我們再怎麼小心也不為過。對動物殘忍的人，對人亦是。）

　　當某人說 "I can't thank you too much."，你如果沒有學過 can't...too... 這個句型，可能會以為他說的是「我無法感謝你太

多」，這樣就鬧了大笑話，他的意思是「我再怎麼感謝你也不為過」，也就是非常地感激。**can't...too...** 表達「再怎樣…也不為過」、「越…越好」、「要格外…」等意義。

例如：

You can't be too careful as walking on the street.（你在街上行走時再怎麼小心也不過。）

We can't praise him too much.（我們再怎麼讚美他也不過。）

這個句子就等於 Our praise for him can never be enough.

One can't learn too much knowledge.（學再多知識也不為過。）

It is impossible to emphasize the importance of health too much.（再怎麼強調健康的重要性也不為過。）

另外要強調的是，can't...too 句型可替換成 can never... enough。

例如：

You can't be too polite.

=You can never be polite enough.（你再怎麼有禮貌也不為過。）

說成 You should be as polite as possible. 也可以，只不過這樣說有點在教訓人家，還是用 can't...too 比較委婉客氣一點。

此外，I can't agree with you more.（我再怎麼同意你也不為過）這個句子只能這麼說，沒辦法套用 can't...too 句型。

英文例句

接著就來看看可以怎樣應用這類句型吧！

✡ **You can't be too careful** in choosing friends because your friends will influence you a lot. You can judge the heart of a friend by his treatment of small animals.

你在選擇朋友時再小心也不為過，因為朋友會對你產生很大的影響。你可以藉由朋友對待小動物的方式來判斷他的心地好壞。

✡ As representatives elected by the people, **lawmakers can't be too humble** in dealing with issues affecting the interests of the general public.

身為人民選出的代表，立法委員在處理影響大眾利益的議題時再謙虛也不為過。

✡ **I can't thank my teacher too much** for giving me encouragement as I feel frustrated about my poor performance in class. It is like saving a drowning man.

我的老師在我對自己課堂上不良的表現感到挫折時給了我鼓勵，我再怎麼感謝他也不為過，那就像是救了一個快要溺水的人。

3 ▶ have to do with

哲學名句

One who makes himself a worm cannot complain afterwards if people step on him. ——*Immanuel Kant*

把自己當成蟲的人不能在事後抱怨別人踩在他的身上。——康德

名句故事

This quote tells us that a man who does not defend his dignity will be despised and stepped on by other people. Such man is compared to a worm, one of the lowest creatures on earth. Be no man's lackey. Be a man and not a lackey.

A lackey is known as a yes-man, who always says "Yes" to others. He is considered to be a servant. No one will respect him. Do not lose your dignity or self-respect as trying to make more friends or be liked by others. A real friend will not treat you as a yes-man.

這句引言告訴我們，一個不捍衛自己的尊嚴的人，會遭到其他人的輕視及踐踏。這樣的人被比喻為蟲，那是地球上最低等的生物之一。不要成為別人的馬屁精。當一個有尊嚴的人，而不是馬屁精。

馬屁精是一種唯唯諾諾的人，只會一直說「是」。他被視為僕人，沒有人會尊敬他。你在嘗試結交更多的朋友或贏得他人的喜歡時，不要失去自己的尊嚴或自我尊重。

句型文法解析

根據哲學名句，我們可以延伸出這樣的句子：The value of a man has much to do with his confidence.（一個人的價值和他的自信有很大的關係。）

再看一個句子，His success has something to do with his hard work.這句話的意思是「他的成功和他的努力工作有點關係」，如果換成 has much to do with 就是「很有關係」，本單元就是要介紹 **have something / little / much / a great deal / nothing to do with** 這個句型。

疑問句則改為 have anything to do with，像是 Does his success have anything to do with his hard work?

否定句則為 do not have anything to do with 或乾脆就用 have nothing to do with。

例如：
He did not have anything to do with the accident.
=He had nothing to do with the accident.（他和那件意外沒有任何關係）

若以哲學名句所引用的 "One who makes himself a worm cannot complain afterwards if people step on him." 來加以改寫，我們可以得出這樣的句子：That people step on a person has much to do with the fact that the person makes himself a worm. 這個句子運用到兩個 that 子句，第一個 that 子句作為主詞，動詞為第三人稱單數的 has，第二個 that 子句則為 the fact 的同位語，兩個 that 子句各自有主詞和動詞，分別是 people 和 step on，以及 the person 和 makes。

這樣的改寫有點累贅，可以簡潔一點，像是：How a man is treated by other people has a great deal to do with how he treats himself.（一個人會如何被其他人對待，和他如何對待自己有很大的關係）。

英文例句

接著就來看看可以怎樣應用這類句型吧！

✡ The accident **has something to do with** human errors, which means it could have been avoided. One who does not follow the standard operation procedure (SOP) tends to make mistakes.
這件意外和人為疏失有點關係，意思是意外本可以避免。不按照標準作業程序的人容易犯錯。

✡ His good relations with friends **have a lot to do with** his being respectful and polite to others. He does not like to use sweet-talking and flattering skills as many people do. 他的好人緣與他的謙遜有禮有關係，他不像許多人一樣喜歡用花言巧語和拍馬屁的技巧。

✡ The billionaire's success **has much to do with** his diligence and hard work. He said he was once as poor as a church mouse.
這位億萬富翁的成功和他的勤奮及辛苦工作有很大的關係，他說他曾經窮得像一隻教堂裡的老鼠。

4 ▶ hoped / wished... to + have p.p

哲學名句

I had to deny knowledge in order to make room for faith.

——Immanuel Kant

我必須否認知識才能為信仰挪出空間。——康德

名句故事

Religious faith has no room for doubt. It is the same for every religion. If you are a Christian, you will not question the Bible. A believer has to deny certain knowledge in order to make room for his faith. Knowledge is about reason, while religion is about faith.

Some Christians have the idea that reason and faith are in conflict. It is impossible to examine every religious belief in a scientific or rational way.

The Bible tells believers to live by faith. Faith, rather than knowledge, is the most important element in religion. It is having confidence in something beyond reason.

宗教信仰不容許有懷疑的空間，不管哪個宗教皆是如此。如果你是基督徒，你就不會質疑聖經。宗教信仰者必須否認某些知識來為自己的信仰挪出空間。知識事關理性，而宗教則事關信仰。

部分基督徒認為理性和信仰之間有衝突。不可能用科學或理性的方法來檢視每一種宗教信仰。

聖經告訴信徒要憑著信仰過生活。宗教最重要的元素是信仰，而不是知識，那是對無法用理性思考加以解釋的事物懷有信心。

> ### 句型文法**解析**

I wished to have denied knowledge to make room for faith. 這個句子改編自本單元的哲學名句，意思是「我真希望拒絕了知識來給信仰挪出空間」，那是與過去事實相反的希望，說話者並沒為了宗教信仰拒絕知識。

這個句子也可以這麼說：I wished that I had denied knowledge to make room for faith. 第二個句型比較常見，也就是 wished（wish 的過去式）+that 子句，that 子句的時態要用過去完成式。

這個句型的規則就是，**如果前面的 wish 用過去式，後面的 that 子句就要用過去完成式，如果 wish 用現在式，that 子句則不一定要用過去完成式，通常是與現在事實相反的簡單過去式。**

例如：
I wish I were a millionaire.（我希望我是個百萬富翁。）
與現在事實相反，所以用 were 而不是 was。不過本單元還是要介紹比較少用的句型，即 wished to have p.p.。

可以套用此句型的動詞還有 intended（intend 的過去式）、meant（mean 的過去式）、hoped（hope 的過去式）、planned（plan 的過去式）、would like、expected（expect 的過去式），但這些動詞不是每個都能套用後面接 that 子句的句型。

英文例句

接著就來看看可以怎樣應用這類句型吧！

✡I **wished to have been** there by your side as you needed me, but I was very busy at the time.

我希望在妳需要我的時候在妳的身邊，可是我當時真的很忙。

✡They **wished to have chosen** another class leader, since the leader chosen by them had his own way and didn't listen to their opinions.

他們希望當時能選出另一位班長，因為他們選出的班長自行其事，不聽他們的意見。

✡He **wished to have studied hard** for the college entrance examination. He also wished to have learned English well.

他希望自己在準備大學聯考時有認真讀書，也希望有把英文學好。

3 儒家思想：
人之初，性本善？性本惡？

1 what's more / worse / better

Ⅲ 哲學名句

When we see men of worth, we should think of equaling them; when we see men of a contrary character, we should turn inwards and examine ourselves. ——*Confucius*

見賢思齊焉，見不賢而內自省也。——孔子

名句故事

This quote encourages us to improve ourselves as we find someone who is better than we are. It also tells us to turn inwards to examine ourselves as we find someone who is not as good as we are.

Those who are doing better than we either financially or academically could be our models. We can learn something from them.

Those who are not as good as us either financially or academically could be examples for we to consider whether we have similar weaknesses.

Self-examination is the most important thing in our lives. It is a necessary process for us to understand ourselves.

這句引言鼓勵我們在看到比自己優秀的人時要提升自我，也告訴我們在看到不如我們的人時，要往內審視檢查自我。

財務上或學術上比我們優秀的人，可以成為我們的模範，我們能從他們學到某些東西。

財務上或學術上不如我們的人，可以讓我們引以為戒，思考是否自己也有類似的弱點。

自我檢視是我們生命中最重要的事情，是瞭解自己必經的程序。

句型文法解析

When we see people who are better than we are, we should think of equaling them; what's more, we should turn inwards and examine ourselves when we see men who are inferior to us. 這個句子是改編自本單元的哲學名句，意思和原句差不多，只不過多加了一個 what's more 這個慣用語作為語氣上的轉折，**what's more** 是「更…，而且」的意思，功能類似的慣用語還有 **what's worse**（更糟的是）和 **what's better**（更棒的是）。

舉例來說，What's better, I got a free gift for buying an early bird ticket.（更棒的是，我因買了早鳥票而獲得免費的禮物。）這個句子也可寫成 What's better was that I got a free ticket for buying an early bird ticket.

Tom is a good student. What's more, he likes to help other people.（湯姆是一個好學生，而且，他還喜歡幫助其他人。）

也可以寫成 What's more is that he likes to help other people；He lost his money and what was worse, his reputation.（他失去了金錢，更糟的是，還失去了名譽。）

He is a good teacher and what is better, a good father.（他是個好老師，更棒的是，還是個好父親。）注意這個句子裡 what was worse 和 what is better，由於沒有縮寫，所以 what 後面的 be 動詞時態要跟著主要子句走，主要子句是現在式就用現在式，過去式則用過去式。

英文例句

接著就來看看可以怎樣應用這類句型吧！

✵ **What's more**, easy access to the Internet has made it possible to receive and send e-mails at any place and at any time. It is really convenient.

更且，上網的便利性讓隨時隨地接收電子郵件變得可能，真的很方便。

✵ The hotel is great. **What's better** is that it has a swimming pool close to the beach.

這家飯店很棒，更棒的是有一座靠近海灘的游泳池。

✵ Many people take exercise regularly to stay healthy. **What's more**, taking exercise can help them stay in shape.

很多人定期運動以保持健康，更且，運動有助於保持身材。

2 ▶ A is to B / as C is to D

哲學名句

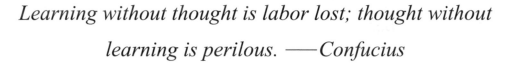

Learning without thought is labor lost; thought without learning is perilous. ——*Confucius*

學而不思則罔，思而不學則殆。——孔子

名句故事

Students learn a lot of things in school, but they never think about what they are learning. Such learning is good for nothing.

On the contrary, students who think a lot without actually learning from teachers or books are likely to make mistakes for insufficient knowledge or understanding.

Learning is a boring process, so a lot of students tend to memorize things without really understanding them. They care only about getting high scores on tests. They forget what they have learned after a test.

Learning and thinking are both important. Learning is the accumulation of knowledge, while thinking is the process of figuring out what has been learned.

學生上學時學到許多東西，但從未想過學的到底是什麼。這樣的學習沒有任何益處。

反之，如果學生想得很多卻沒有真正地從老師或書本學習到知識，可能會因知識或瞭解不足而犯錯。

學習是一個無聊的過程，所以很多學生傾向只記憶知識，而不去理解。他們只在乎考試得高分，考完試後就忘了所學的。

學習和思考都重要，學習是知識的累積，思考則是理解所學的一種過程。

句型文法解析

英文有的句型複雜到有點像是數學公式，譬如 A is to B as C is to D 和 A is to B what C is to D：Reading is to the mind as exercise is to the body.（閱讀之於心靈猶如運動之於身體。）

Reading is to the mind what exercise is to the body. 是一樣的意思，這種句型是用 as 和 what 來連接兩個對比的句子；Thought is to learning as digestion is to eating.（思考之於學習猶如消化之於吃東西。）這個句子改寫自本單元的哲學名句，剛好可以套用這個句型；前兩個例句也可以寫成 As exercise is to the body, so is reading to the mind. 和 As digestion is to eating, so is thought to learning.

注意 **A is to B as C is to D** 要改成 **As C is to D, so is A to B**。

Smile is to mankind as / what sunshine is to flowers.（微笑之於人猶如陽光之於花朵。）

Twelve is to three as four is to one.（12 之於 3 猶如 4 之於 1。）

Air is to man what water is to fish.（空氣之於人猶如水之於魚。）

Music does for the mind as vegetables do for the body.
（音樂對於心靈的作用猶如蔬菜對於身體的作用。）

要注意，這種對比的句型不見得只有用 be 動詞，也可以用一般動詞，但機率比較少，且難度比較高。

 英文例句

接著就來看看可以怎樣應用這類句型吧！

✡ **Table tennis is to China as soccer is to Britain.** Most of the best table tennis players in the world are Chinese.
桌球之於中國猶如足球之於英國。世界最佳的桌球選手大多是中國人。

✡ **Typhoon is to Taiwan as hurricane is to the U.S.** Taiwan is hit by three to four typhoons each year.
颱風之於台灣猶如颶風之於美國，台灣每年遭受三到四次颱風襲擊。

✡ **Freud is to psychoanalysis as Shakespeare is to English literature.** Psychoanalysis was founded by Freud. Its aim is to release repressed emotions.
佛洛伊德之於精神分析猶如莎士比亞之於英國文學，精神分析是佛洛伊德所創，目的是釋放被壓抑的情緒。

3 ▶ by + 名詞

|||| 哲學名句

⤜⤛⤜⤛

By nature, men are nearly alike; by practice, they get to be wide apart. ——*Confucius*

性相近也，習相遠也。——孔子

名句故事

All humans are equal when born. They are similar from the very beginning. It is the education and the environment that make them become different from each other later in life.

Despite receiving the same education, people often do things differently. Some of them do things better than others. They may be more intelligent, but that does not explain it all.

They are in an environment which makes them constantly change and grow. They do not learn all the things from their school teachers. They also learn from the environment. What's more important, they put into practice what they have learned. They are thus able to become different.

所有人類在出生時皆是平等的，一開始都很類似。是教育和環境讓他們後來變得彼此不同。

儘管接受同樣的教育，人們經常用不同的方式做事情。有些人做事做得比較好，或許是因為比較聰明，但那不足以說明一切。

他們身處在一個讓他們經常改變和成長的環境，並不是只從學校老師學習，也從周遭的環境學習。更重要的是，他們把所學的東西付諸實現，因此變得不同。

句型文法解析

　　片語 **by nature** 是「本性上、天生地」的意思，而 by practice 則是「經由練習、經由實踐」的意思，不要與 in practice（實務上、實際上、在實踐中），例如：He is a doctor in practice.（他是一個執業醫生）我們就不會說 He is a doctor by practice. 那樣意思會變成他經由練習成為醫生，不符合英文的慣用原則，所以不能這麼說。

　　Our memory can be improved by practice.（我們可經由練習改善記憶。）本單元要介紹 **by+名詞**所構成的片語，最常見的有 by bus、by train、by plane、by car，這是表達交通方式。

　　例如：He goes to school by bus.（他搭公車上學。）
也可以說 He takes a bus to school. 但不如 go by bus 簡潔。

　　We went to Taipei by train yesterday.
　　=We took a train to Taipei yesterday.（我們昨天搭火車到台北。）

　　We can go to Hualien by plane.
　　=We can take a plane to Hualien.（我們可以搭飛機到花蓮。）

　　He usually goes to the office by car, but sometimes on foot.（他通常開車到辦公室，不過有時用走的。）

用走的是 on foot，不是 by foot，簡單一點就說：

He sometimes walks to the office.（他有時候走路去辦公室。）

He gets to the supermarket by bike.（他騎腳踏車到超市）。

英文例句

接著就來看看可以怎樣應用這類句型吧！

✡ Humans are **by nature** social animals and can't live without society. He who lives alone will not live long.

人類天生是社會動物，無法脫離社會生活。獨自生活的人活不長久。

✡ We plan to go to Hualien **by plane**, but the plane tickets cost too much. It is much cheaper to go there **by train**.

我們計畫搭飛機到花蓮，可是飛機票很貴，搭火車去便宜很多。

✡ Many people now leave their cars at home and commute to work **by bus**. They save a lot of money and bring less air pollution to the world.

很多人現在把車子留在家裡，改搭巴士通勤上下班。他們省下很多錢並為世界減少空氣污染。

4 ▶ that's why / how

Ⅲ 哲學名句

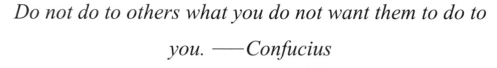

Do not do to others what you do not want them to do to you. ——*Confucius*

己所不欲，勿施於人。——孔子

名句故事

This is a golden rule that we have to keep in mind. Some people like to criticize others. They do not understand how much harm their criticism can do to other people. Their tolerance for different opinions is very low, which makes them become easily angered.

When they criticize someone else, they throw negative energy at that person without realizing that they are doing something bad.

When you encounter such people, you had better not be offended by them. You have the option of not responding to them. If you talk back to them, you are acting like them. Make them feel that you are different from them.

這是一個我們必須謹記在心的金科玉律。某些人喜歡批評他人，他們不知道他們的批評會對其他人造成多大的傷害。他們對不同意見的容忍度很低，因此容易被激怒。

當他們批評某人時，就是把負面能量往那個人的身上丟，不瞭解自己正在做一件壞事。

當你碰到這種人時，最好不要被他們激怒。你可以選擇不回應他們，如果回應，就會和他們一樣。要讓他們覺得你和他們不同。

句型文法解析

You had better not do to others what you do not them to do to you. That's why you need to be careful about what you do. （你最好不要對他人做出你不想讓他們對你做的事，那是你要謹慎行事的原因）這個句子改編自本單元的哲學名句，不過納入了 **that's why** 這個句型，就是「因為什麼緣故」的意思。

也有人說 **that's the reason why**，多了 the reason，但有沒有 the reason 並沒有差，直接說 that's why 就好，如果要保留 the reason，後面的 why 可以省略，成為 **that's the reason**。

例如：

That's why he did it.

=That's the reason why he did it. （那是他做那件事的原因。）

That's (the reason) why people admire you.（那是人們崇拜你的原因。）

類似的句型有 that's how 和 that's the way how，意思是那是怎樣達成的。

例如：

That's how I spend my money.（那是我用錢的方式）

也可以說 That's the way how I spend my money.

That's how it works. (那是它運作的方式。)

That's how he gets the girl. (那是他把到妹的方法。)

That's how to make a cake. (那是製作蛋糕的方式。)

how 後面可以接句子或不定詞片語，how to make a cake 就相當於 how you can make a cake.

1

2

3 儒家思想

4

英文例句

接著就來看看可以怎樣應用這類句型吧！

✡ Henry stayed up last night to finish his report. **That's why** he was late for work this morning.
亨利昨晚熬夜完成報告，那是他今天早上上班遲到的原因。

✡ We did not know that the teacher was sick. **That's why** he sometimes lost his temper and blamed us for small things.
我們不曉得老師生病了，那是他有時發脾氣並為了小事罵我們的原因。

✡ Baseball is a very interesting and exciting sport. **That's why** so many people like to play baseball or watch others play the game.
棒球是一種非常有趣和令人興奮的運動，那是那麼多人喜歡打棒球或看人打棒球的原因。

5 ▶ those people who

🏛 哲學名句

Look not at what is contrary to propriety; listen not to what is contrary to propriety; speak not what is contrary to propriety; make no movement which is contrary to propriety. ——*Confucius*

非禮勿視，非禮勿聽，非禮勿言，非禮勿動。——孔子

📖 名句故事

This quote tells people not to look at, listen to, speak about, and do what does not conform to propriety. Propriety is defined as behavior that is accepted as socially correct or morally correct and proper. It also means the state or quality of being correct and proper.

Confucius emphasized the importance of propriety

because he wanted to restore the rites of the Zhou dynasty.

He also advocated the thought of "benevolence," which he defined as "the love of people." As asked about the meaning of benevolence by one of his disciples, Confucius said, "Benevolence is to subdue one's self and restore to propriety." In other words, propriety is necessary for the development of benevolence.

這句引言告訴人們不要看、聽、談論、及做不符合禮的事情。禮被定義為社交上正確或道德上正確及恰當的行為，也指正確及恰當的狀態或性質。孔子強調禮的重要性，因為他想要恢復周朝的禮儀。

孔子也提倡「仁」這個思想，按照他的解釋，仁就是「愛人民」。當一位弟子問及仁的意義時，孔子説，「仁就是克己復禮」。換句話説，禮是發展仁所必需。

句型文法解析

Those who act contrary to propriety are not gentlemen.
People who act contrary to propriety are not gentlemen.
They who act contrary to propriety are not gentlemen.
He who (anyone who) acts contrary to propriety is not a gentleman.

Whoever acts contrary to propriety is not a gentleman.

Such as act contrary to propriety are not gentlemen.

這幾個句子都對，只是不同句型的替換，意思是「行事違禮的人非君子。」裡面最常見的是 **those who** 和 **people who**。都是主格的用法，受格怎麼辦？

例如：

He prays for those whom he loves.（他為他所愛的人禱告。）

所有格的用法則為：Happy are those whose wishes are granted.（願望得到恩准之人是高興的。）

People who live in glass houses should not throw stones.（住在玻璃屋裡的人不該丟石頭。）

這是一句很有名的諺語。

Blessed are the meek. The meek are those who are gentle and humble.（溫順的人有福了，溫順的人是溫和謙虛之人。）

聖經的英本版本中經常有 those who 的句型。

He who laughs last laughs hardest.（最後一個笑的人笑得最大力。）

這也是一個俗諺，像是中國話所說的「別笑得太早」。

He who perseveres goes far.（堅忍的人走得長遠。）

改成 Those who persevere go far. 亦可。

Anyone who has never made a mistake has never tried

anything new.（一個人從未犯錯是因為從未嘗試新的事物）。

英文例句

接著就來看看可以怎樣應用這類句型吧！

❈ **Those who** know little talk a lot, and people who know much talk little. It means the same when you say, "Half full water bucket sounds louder."
懂得少的人話很多，懂得多的人話很少，當你說，「半桶水響叮噹」，也是一樣的意思。

❈ **He who knows** how to stay healthy is optimistic, and he who is optimistic has everything.
知道如何保持健康的人是樂觀的，樂觀的人擁有一切。

❈ **They who** don't know the value of a book never appreciate the fun of reading. Reading is a mind-opening activity.
不懂得書的價值的人從未領略閱讀的樂趣，閱讀是一種開啟心靈的活動。

6 ▶ 介系詞 +hand

If a man takes no thought about what is distant, he will find sorrow near at hand. ——*Confucius*

人無遠慮，必有近憂。——孔子

名句故事

The teaching is about preparing for a rainy day. If you do not plan for the future, you will find problems sooner or later.

Unexpected events can happen to anyone at any time. They could be car accidents, job changes, and investment failures.

In the case of a car accident, if you have already bought

car insurance, you will not be at a loss about what to do. You are financially prepared for an unexpected happening. Your insurance agent will also tell you how to deal with it.

That's why we should prepare for a rainy day, even if we do not know when it will rain.

這個教誨是告訴人要未雨綢繆。如果對未來沒有規劃，遲早就會發現問題。

意外事件會隨時發生在任何一個人身上，像是車禍、換工作、及投資失利。

以車禍來說，如果你已經買了車險，就不會茫然不知所措。你在財務上做好對意外發生的準備。你的保險員也會告訴你該如何處理。

那是我們應該未雨綢繆的理由，即便我們不知何時會下雨。

句型文法解析

英文諺語 A bird in the hand is worth two in the bush.（一鳥在手勝於兩鳥在林。）用到 in the hand（在手中）這個片語，不過現代英文用 **in hand** 來表達同樣的意思，像是 a project in hand（手中的一項計畫），have cash in hand / on hand（手上有現金）。

本單元介紹的文法就是**介系詞+hand** 所構成的片語，像是 **in hand**、**at hand**、**on hand**，哲學名句裡的 **sorrow at hand** 表示距離很近的憂慮，就是近憂，只能用 at hand，不能説成 sorrow in hand 或 sorrow on hand。**at hand** 是「即將到來、在附近」的意思。

例如：
Winter is close at hand.（冬天即將到來。）

She always keeps a dictionary at hand.（她總是在手邊準備一本字典。）

He has a pencil at hand.（他手邊有一支鉛筆）。

on hand 是「在手上、尚待處理、在場」的意思，表示「在手上」時可以和 in hand 互換，像是前面提到的手上有現金。

I have a lot of work on hand.（我還有很多工作要做。）

My assistant will be on hand to help you. （我的助手會在現場幫你。）

in hand 除了「在手上」的意思外，還有「正在進行、掌握住的」，例如：The police took the situation in hand.（警察控制了情況）。

英文例句

接著就來看看可以怎樣應用這類句型吧！

✡ If you don't have cash **in hand**, you can pay by credit card. You can pay for the car in monthly installments.
如果你沒有現金，可以用信用卡付款，分期支付這個車子的費用。

✡ Since the summer vacation is **at hand**, Mr. Wang plans to take a trip to Japan with his son, who is a junior high school student.
由於暑假即將來臨，王先生打算帶就讀國中的兒子到日本旅遊。

✡ Rescue dogs are **on hand** to help search and rescue teams find survivors in the earthquake.
搜救犬在現場幫助搜救隊找尋地震中的生還者。

7 ▶ the + 形容詞

哲學名句

The wise find pleasure in water; the virtuous find pleasure in hills. The wise are active; the virtuous are tranquil. The wise are joyful; the virtuous are long-lived.

——Confucius

智者樂水，仁者樂山。智者動，仁者靜。智者樂，仁者瘦。

——孔子

名句故事

Mountains and water play important roles in Chinese philosophy. The word for landscape in Chinese is shanshui, "mountain-water." Either in paintings or in philosophical works, the Chinese always try to express certain connections with mountains or water.

Traditionally, water is associated with wise people, while mountains are associated with virtuous people. The wise are active like water and the virtuous are tranquil like mountains.

Our wisdom is constantly changing and moving like water. Our morals are always the same, which is the reason why virtuous people are considered to be long-lived. The Chinese want to be close to mountains and water, showing their inclination toward wisdom and high moral standards.

山和水在中國哲學中扮演重要的角色。中文裡用來表達風景的詞語就是山水二字。不管是在圖畫還是哲學作品裡，中國人總是試圖表達與山或水的某種關連。

傳統上，水與智者有關，山則與有德行之人有關。智者像水一樣活躍，有德行者則像山一樣寧靜。

我們的智慧像水一樣經常地改變和移動，我們的德行則保持不變，有德行者因此常被視為長壽者。中國人想要親近山和水，顯示他們對智慧和高道德的嚮往。

句型文法解析

本單元的哲學名句提到 the wise 和 the virtuous，就是指 wise people（智者）和 virtuous people（仁者），文法結構為 the+形容詞來代表某一種人，像是 the rich（富人）、the poor（窮人）、the old（老人）、the young（年輕人）、the disabled（殘障者）、the unemployed（失業者）、the blind（盲者）等，**既然代表某一種人，動詞就要用第三人稱複數。**

例如：
The rich are not always happy.（有錢人不一定快樂。）

The government should take care of the homeless.（政府應該照顧遊民。）

The young should help the old if necessary.（年輕人應該在必要時幫助老年人。）

The unemployed are those who are jobless.（失業者就是沒有工作的人。）

The brave are always the first to die.（勇者總是第一個死。）

The young are the future.（年輕人就是未來。）
說 The future belongs to the young.（未來屬於年輕人。）也可以。

It is not only the old who are wise.（不是年老者才有智慧。）
這句話取自聖經，古代人早就體會這一點，也算是一種智慧。

The wise win before they fight, while the ignorant fight to win.（智者不戰而勝，愚者為勝而戰。）
這是孫子的名言之一。

接著就來看看可以怎樣應用這類句型吧！

✤ **The rich** are not always happy, and the poor are not always unhappy. It varies with each individual.
有錢的人不總是快樂，窮人也不總是不快樂，這要因人而異。

✤ **The brave** might not be physically strong. They are mentally strong. They will fight for justice and freedom.
勇敢的人或許不是身體強壯，而是心靈強壯，他們會為了正義和自由而戰。

✤ Some people say that **the young** are slaves to dreams. Is it possible for young people to live without dreams? Living without dreams is like living an empty life.
某些人說年輕人是夢想的奴隸。年輕人有可能沒有夢想嗎？沒有夢想就像是過著空虛的生命一般。

8 what with... and (what with)...

哲學名句

Those who are born with knowledge are the best; those who acquire knowledge through learning are second best. Those who learn because of difficulties are less good. The worst are those who do not try to learn even in the face of difficulties. ——Confucius

生而知之者，上也；學而知之者，次也；困而學之者，又其次也；困而不學，民斯為下矣！——孔子

名句故事

People born with knowledge are those who take the initiative to pursue knowledge at a young age. It does not mean that they are geniuses. They are just able to find out the answers to their problems.

They are considered to be the best because they teach themselves without having to be taught by others. They could learn from others what they do not know, but it is an active learning process different from passive learning patterns most commonly seen in school.

Most people fall into the category of second best because they do not learn as actively as the first type of people, who are few and far between.

生而知之者是指年紀很小就會主動追求知識的人,這並不表示他們是天才,他們只是能找出問題的解答。

他們被視為上等人,因為他們自己就能教自己,不需要別人來教他們。他們可以從別人身上學到自己不知道的東西,但這是一種主動學習的過程,不同於學校裡常見的被動學習模式。

多數人屬於第二等人,因為他們主動學習的程度不如少之又少的第一種人。

句型文法解析

按照本單元要介紹的文法概念，我們可以把哲學名句改為：What with a lack of interest in learning and what with an unwillingness to learn even in the face of difficulties, Peter finds it hard for him to graduate from college.（部分由於對學習缺乏興趣，部分由於即便碰到困難也不願學習，彼得發現很難從大學畢業）。這個句子帶出 what with（因為，由於）這個慣用語的用法。

本單元介紹的 **what with** 通常是成雙出現，也就是和前面的改寫句子一樣是前後出現，表示部分的原因。

例如：

What with love of nature and what with air pollution, Henry has decided to move to a rural area.

（部分因為愛好自然，部分因為空氣污染，亨利決定搬到鄉村地區）。

除了 what with 外，也有 what by，表示手段。

例如：

What by hard work and what by perseverance, he finally succeeded.（部分是藉著努力工作，部分是藉著堅持不懈，他終於成功）。

類似的句型還有 what of...and what of、what for...what for、what through...what through、what between...what between 等，但這些句型現在比較少用，知道一下就好。

英文例句

接著就來看看可以怎樣應用這類句型吧！

❈ **What with** walking a long distance and **what with** having not enough water to drink, I am so exhausted to be unable to walk any farther.

部分因為走了一大段路，部分因為沒有足夠的水喝，我精疲力竭到無法再走了。

❈ **What with** the high cost of living in Taipei and **what with** the economic slowdown in recent years, double income families are now quite common in Taipei.

部分因為台北的高生活水平，部分因為這些年來的經濟停滯，雙薪家庭現在在台北很常見。

❈ **What with** illness and **what with** worsening working conditions, Mr. Lin decided to retire early to take better care of himself.

部分因為生病，部分因為工作條件惡化，林先生決定提早退休以便好好照顧自己。

1 as... as

🎼 哲學名句

Take care of elderly people in general as you take care of your own parents. Care for other people's children as your own. ——Mencius

老吾老以及人之老，幼吾幼以及人之幼。——孟子

📖 名句故事

The quote is about universal love for all people. If you can take good care of your parents and children, why can't you extend the same love to other people?

It is easier said than done. People are often too occupied with their own family matters to care about other people. It does not mean that they do not have compassion for all human beings. They are just too busy.

Under the circumstances, they might choose to donate money to charity organizations, which will use the money to help those in need. It is one way of demonstrating your love for all people. There are still many other ways for you to choose from.

這句引言論及博愛。如果你能照顧好自己的父母和小孩,為何不能把這樣的愛擴及到其他人?

說很容易,做很難。人們通常太忙於自己的家務事,以致於無暇照顧到其他人。這不是說他們沒有博愛之心,他們只是太忙了。

在這樣的情況下,他們可以選擇捐錢給慈善團體來幫助有需要的人。這是展現博愛的一種方式,還有許多其他種方式可供你選擇。

句型文法解析

博愛精神有許多表現方式，哲學名句也可以改寫成這樣：Be as kind and helpful to others as to your family members. 或 Treat others as you do your family members. 句子用到本單元要介紹的 as...as 句型（和…一樣）。

先介紹這個句型的基本款，也就是在兩個 **as** 之間加上形容詞或副詞，如果第一個 **as** 之前是 **be** 動詞，**as** 後面就用形容詞，如果不是 **be** 動詞而是一般動詞，就用副詞。

例如：

Jim is as smart as Tom.（吉姆和湯姆一般聰明。）

Susan can sing as well as Helen.（蘇珊可以唱得和海倫一樣好）。

接下來是進階款，就是在 as...as 之間加上形容詞和名詞。

例如：

I have as many books as she.（我的書和她的一樣多。）

這是表達相同的數目，如果要表達倍數，就要把倍數放在第一個 as 之前。

例如：

I have twice as many books as she.（我的書的數量是她的兩倍。）

This car is about twice as large as that one.（這部車約是那

部車的兩倍大）。

英文例句

接著就來看看可以怎樣應用這類句型吧！

✡ Paul's essay is **as good as** anyone can imagine, but he is not good at expressing his ideas orally.

保羅的文章說有多好就有多好，可是他不善於口頭表達。

✡ John can run **as fast as** the best runner in his school, but he did not perform that well in the contest.

約翰能跑得和全校最快的跑者一樣快，可是他在比賽中的表現並沒有那麼好。

✡ As Taiwan's largest city, New Taipei City is not **as prosperous as** its neighboring Taipei City, which bustles with business activities.

新北市是台灣最大的城市，卻沒有像隔壁的台北市一樣繁榮，台北市可是有著許多的商業活動。

2 ▶ as... as possible / one can

哲學名句

Only an educated man is able to keep a fixed heart under the condition of having no fixed property. As to the common people, if they do not have fixed property, they are unable to maintain a fixed heart. If they do not have a fixed heart, there is nothing that they will not do, such as criminal, immoral and lavish acts. ——*Mencius*

無恆產而有恆心者，惟士為能。若民，則無恆產，因無恆心。

苟無恆心，放辟邪侈，無不為已。——孟子

名句故事

An educated man was highly respected in ancient China. He took pride in his knowledge. He did not aspire to own fixed property such as land. Despite having no material comforts, he could still maintain a fixed heart.

By contrast, the common people, if without fixed property, would not be able to keep a fixed heart. They would change according to the change of circumstances and follow no fixed rules.

It was the difference between an educated man and the ordinary people. But things are different nowadays. Educated men were extremely few in ancient times. There are now few if any people who have not been educated, however.

士在古代中國受到高度的重視，他以擁有知識為榮，不渴望擁有土地之類的固定資產。儘管沒有物質上的享受，士仍能保有恆定之心。

相較之下，一般人民若是沒有固定資產，就無法保持恆定之心。他們隨著情況的改變而改變，不會遵循固定的規矩。

這是士和一般人的差別。但現在可不一樣。古代受教育的人很少，現在沒受過教育的人就算有也是很少。

句型文法解析

　　古代的士是富貴不能淫貧賤不能移，據此我們可以把哲學名句改寫為：An educated man will try as hard as he can to keep a fixed heart even if he does not live a materially comfortable life.（士將盡其可能保持恆定之心，儘管並沒有過著舒適的物質生活）。這個句子帶出本單元要介紹的 **as...as one can** 或 **as...as possible**（盡可能）句型。

　　大家應該都見過或聽過 ASAP 這個縮寫，其實就是 as soon as possible（快一點）的意思，常見的類似例句還有 Take as much exercise as possible / as you can.（盡量多運動），Drink as much water as possible/as you drink.（盡可能多喝水）。

　　as...as 之間可以放入名詞，如前面的兩個例子，也可以放入形容或副詞。

　　例如：
Be as careful as possible.（盡可能小心。）
Run as fast as you can.（盡可能地快跑。）

　　前一個句子用形容詞，因為動詞是 be 動詞，而後一個句子則用副詞，因為動詞是一般動詞 run。另外，如果用的是 as...as one can 句型，後面的 can 要跟著前面的時態做改變：He tries to work as hard as he can. / He tried to work as hard as he could.

英文例句

接著就來看看可以怎樣應用這類句型吧！

✡ If you want to get good grades, you need to study **as hard as you can**.

如果你想要得到好成績，就要盡量用功讀書。

✡ The doctor asks Mr. Wang to be **as relaxed as possible** so that his health conditions could improve. But Mr. Wang says that he does not know how to relax himself.

醫生要王先生盡可能放鬆，這樣才能改善健康狀況。可是王先生說他不知道如何放鬆自己。

✡ It is important to save **as much money as possible** at younger ages, or there will not be enough money for retirement.

年輕時盡可能存多一點錢很重要，不然就沒有足夠的錢退休。

3 be ashamed of

哲學名句

A person must not be without shame. If you are not ashamed of your shamelessness, you will not feel ashamed at all. ——Mencius

人不可以無恥。無恥之恥，無恥矣。——孟子

名句故事

　　A man without a sense of shame does not feel guilty about any wrongdoing. Generally speaking, it is hard to find a man totally without a sense of shame. Even the most shameless man will feel embarrassed about something he does. Such embarrassment indicates that he still cares about what people thinks of him.

If there is a man who does not seem to be ashamed of his improper behavior, he might be pretending to be impervious because he does not want to look weak.

We had better not provoke him at this juncture since he might lose control of himself. Just give him some time to calm down and reflect on his own behavior.

1
2
3 儒家思想
4

沒有羞恥心的人不會對自己做的錯事有罪惡感。一般說來，很難找到完全沒有羞恥心的人，即使最無恥的人也會對自己做的事感到難為情。這種難為情代表他仍然在乎人們對他的看法。

如果某人看起來並沒有因自己的不恰當行為而感到羞恥，他可能是故意裝得無動於衷，因為他不想表現出懦弱的樣子。

我們最好不要在這個時候激怒他，因為他或許會失去控制。給他一點時間冷靜下來並反省自己的行為。

句型文法解析

　　哲學名句用到 **be ashamed of**（以…為恥）這個慣用語，本單元除了介紹 be ashamed of 外，還包括意思或結構類似的用語。

　　be ashamed of 後面可以接動名詞或 **what** 所引導的字句，也可以接複合人稱代名詞（或稱反身代名詞）。

　　例如：

He is ashamed of what he did.（他以自己所做的事為恥。）

I am ashamed of having said something bad.（我以說了一些不好的話為恥。）

You should be ashamed of yourself.（你應該為自己感到羞恥。）

I was ashamed of myself for losing my temper.（我為自己發了脾氣感到羞恥。）

　　be shy of 在結構上類似 be ashamed of，可是意思不是表面上的意思，讓我們來看一個例句：The final tally was 57 to 36, three votes shy of the 60 needed for the bill to pass.（最後的統計是 57 票對 36 票，還差三票才能達到法案通過所需的 60 票門檻。）

　　這裡的 be shy of 是缺少的意思，不是害羞，如果沒碰過這個詞語，可能一開始會楞在那裡。be shy of 也有害羞的意思，但現在比較常用來表示缺少。

英文例句

接著就來看看可以怎樣應用這類句型吧！

✡ We should not **be ashamed of** having poor friends since it is not their fault to be poor.

我們不應該以有窮朋友為恥，因為窮又不是他們的錯。

✡ A man who **is not ashamed of** having said something bad to other people tends to make the same mistake again and again.

一個不以對他人說過不好的話為恥的人，通常會一直犯同樣的錯誤。

✡ The 64 to 36 vote **was** two votes **shy of** the passage of the bill, which was a shame indeed.

投票結果是 64 票贊成 36 反對，還差兩票就可以通過法案，實在可惜。

4 ▶ not so much... as...

 **哲學名句**

The people are the most important element in a state. The government comes second and the ruler is the least important. ——Mencius

民為貴，社稷次之，君為輕。——孟子

名句故事

Mencius' idea that the people are more important than the government and the ruler is very much like what all modern democratic countries believe in. It is amazing that such democratic idea had existed in ancient China.

As we know it, a democratic system is for the people and by the people. The government serves the needs of the people, while the ruler takes the opinions of the people as the basis of his policy.

China had been ruled by emperors for thousands of years. These emperors did not have to listen to the people. They just had their own way without having to care about the needs of the people. A democratic ruler is totally different.

孟子這套人民比政府及統治者重要的理念，非常類似所有現代民主國家所信仰的。這種民主理念曾出現在古代中國，實在讓人感到吃驚。

如我們所知，民主制度是為了人民而存在，也要由人民來治理。政府服務人民的需求，而統治者則以人民的意見作為政策的基礎。

中國被皇帝統治了數千年，這些皇帝不需要聽從人民的意見，他們自行其事，不用顧慮人民的需求。民主制度的統治者則完全不同。

句型文法解析

　　根據本單元要介紹的句型，哲學名句可改寫為：The government is not as important as the people, while the ruler is the least important.（政府沒有人民來得重要，而統治者則最不重要）或是 The government does not have so much importance as the people.（政府的重要性不如人民），第二個句子用到 **not so much...as** 句型。這個句型的 **so much** 後面可以接名詞、介系詞片語、動詞。

　　例如：

He is not so much a businessman as an opportunist. =He is an opportunist rather than a businessman.（與其說他是個生意人，不如說他是個機會主義者。）

The company's success lies not so much in sale promotion as in leadership.（這家公司的成功與其說是在於促銷活動，不如說是領導有方。）

Technology does not so much make people become smarter as make machines become smarter.（與其說科技讓人們變得比較聰明，不如說讓機器變得比較聰明。）

　　這個句子也可以寫成 Technology does not make people become smarter so much as make machines become smarter.

　　或 Technology makes machines become smarter rather

than makes people become smarter.

　　列出這幾個可以互換的句型，只是為了讓大家多一點瞭解，如果覺得不好掌握，就選擇其中一種用就好。

英文例句

接著就來看看可以怎樣應用這類句型吧！

✡ A white lie is **not so much a lie as** an effort to prevent the listener from being hurt or keep him from knowing something that he might not be happy to know.
與其說善意的謊言是謊言，不如說是為了不讓聽者受到傷害或聽到不想聽的事情所做的努力。

✡ The Internet does **not so much** bring people together virtually as push them away physically.
與其說網際網路拉近人們在虛擬空間裡的距離，不如說加大他們在現實空間裡的距離。

✡ The value of a book depends **not so much** on its subject matter as on the reader's response to it.
與其說一本書的價值是在於主題，不如說是讀者的反應。

5 ▶ the + 形容詞最高級 + of / among

哲學名句

I am well-prepared for all things. There is no greater joy than to reflect myself and find I am sincere. As I conduct myself according to the principle of reciprocity, I am moving closer to humaneness that I seek to realize.

——Mencius

萬物皆備於我矣。反身而誠，樂莫大焉。

彊恕而行，求仁莫近焉。——孟子

名句故事

It is very difficult to find a proper English word for 仁(Ren), which is one of the most important ideas in Confucianism and Mencius's interpretation of Confucianism.

According to Wikipedia, Ren is a Confucian virtue denoting the good feeling that a virtuous man feels when he is altruistic. It means that Ren is a kind of good feeling when one tries to help or bring advantages to others. It is an interesting way of interpreting Ren.

A selfish man cannot experience Ren, since he will not act in an altruistic way. He cares only about himself. Ren is basically about the relationship between two persons, who have to help each other to maintain the relationship.

很難為仁這個字找到合適的英文字，在孔子的學說及孟子對孔子學說的闡述中，仁是最重要的理念之一。

根據維基百科，仁是一種儒家德行，代表有德行之人在做出利他行為時所得到的美好感覺，意思就是在幫助他人或為他人帶來好處時所體驗到的美好感覺。這種對仁的闡述很有意思。

自私的人感受不到仁，因為他不會做出利他行為，只會關心自己。仁基本上就是兩人之間的關係，雙方必須彼此協助才能維持關係。

句型文法解析

　　配合本單元要介紹的文法句型，可以把哲學名句改寫為：The greatest joy among all that I have experienced in my pursuit of humaneness is self-examination.（在我追求仁的過程中，所經歷的最大快樂就是自省）。這個句子用到 **the + 形容詞最高級 + of / among + 複數名詞 + in + 地方**此一句型。

　　這個句型並不難，但要注意形容詞最高級的變化，規則變化用 the most 表示最高級，這類形容詞大多是兩個音節或三個音節以上，字尾以 ly 結尾的副詞也是以 the most 表示最高級。

例如：

the most careful 和 the most selfish（兩個音節的形容詞）
the most important 和 the most difficult（三個音節的形容詞）
the most quickly（以 ly 結尾的副詞）

　　這些是規則的變化，還有不規則的變化，像是 good / best、well / best、bad / worst、big / biggest、happy / happiest、pretty / prettiest 等。

舉例來說：

She is the best student in our class.（她是我們班上最好的學生。）
He is the most popular among the new employees.（他在新來的雇員裡是最受歡迎的。）

英文**例句**

接著就來看看可以怎樣應用這類句型吧！

✡ As **the most beautiful girl in her class**, Helen also studies hard to show that what she has is not just a beautiful look.

身為班上最美麗的女孩，海倫也以用功讀書來證明她擁有的不只是美麗外貌。

✡ A Taiwan-made smartphone has been rated as one of **the most user-friendly among** smartphones sold around the world.

一款台灣製造智慧手機被評定為全世界智慧手機中對使用者最友善的機型之一。

✡ John is **the fastest runner in his class**, but he failed to win a medal for his class in a recent 100-meter race.

約翰在班上跑得最快，可是在最近的百米賽跑中，他未能為班上贏得一面獎牌。

1 ▶ the + 比較級 , the + 比較級

 **哲學名句**

There must be an original source for all things that arise. The honor or disgrace that a person receives reflects his virtue. ——Hsun Tzu

物類之起，必有所始；榮辱之來，必象其德。——荀子

名句故事

For Christians, God is the source of all things. God is the creator of all living creatures.

For the Chinese, however, the source of all things is not a religious god. It is the way of nature that makes possible the existence of all creatures and the happening of all things. It involves a cause and effect relationship.

A man who is honored by the general public must have done something good. He is a man of virtue. His deeds reflect his inner soul.

Likewise, a man who has been disgraced must have done something bad. He has to take the consequences of his own deeds.

對基督徒來說，上帝是萬事萬物的起源，上帝創造了所有生物。

然對中國人來說，萬事萬物的起源不是宗教上的神，自然之道才是所有生物得以生存及所有事情所以發生的原因，其中包括了因果關係。

一個被大眾尊崇的人，一定是做了好事，他是個有德行之人，他的行為反映出內在的靈魂。

同樣的，一個受到羞辱的人，一定做了壞事，他必須承擔自己行為的後果。

句型文法解析

按照哲學名句，我們可以衍生出這樣的句子：The more you are honored by other people, the better man you are considered to be.（其他人對你的尊敬越多，你在他們眼中就越好）。句子用到了本單元要介紹的 **the+比較級, the+比較級**（越…越…）句型。

這種句型最常見的例子有 The sooner, the better.（越快越好）及 The bigger, the better.（越大越好），我們要介紹的不是這種簡化形式，而是完整的句子。

例如：
The hotter the weather is, the better the sales of ice cream will become.（天氣越熱，冰淇淋的銷量會越好。）

The harder you work, the greater your chance of promotion will be.（你工作越努力，你升遷的機會就越大。）

the 後面的比較級可以是形容詞或副詞，若是形容詞就是主詞補語，若是副詞就是作為修飾動詞之用。

第一個句子原來應該這麼說：If the weather is hotter, the sales of ice cream will become better.

而第二個句子則為：If you work harder, your chance of promotion will be greater. 簡單來說，就是一種倒裝句，用來加強

語氣之用。

英文例句

接著就來看看可以怎樣應用這類句型吧！

✡ **The more** a man gets, **the more** he wants. It shows that greed is part of human nature.

人得到越多就會想要更多，這顯示貪婪是人性的一部份。

✡ **The more** time you take to repay the money you borrow from a bank, **the more** interest you pay to the bank.

你花越多的時間來返還從銀行借出的錢，就要支付更多的利息給銀行。

✡ **The more** beautiful a woman is, the lonelier she is. But it does not mean that the less physically attractive a woman is, **the more** popular she is.

女人越美麗，就越孤單，但這並不表示外表越不吸引人，就越受歡迎。

2 ▶ 副詞片語

󰳕 哲學名句

You can't walk a distance of thousand miles unless you walk step by step. Rivers and seas can't be formed unless they are gradually enlarged by small tributaries.

——Hsun Tzu

故不積蹞步，無以至千里；不積小流，無以成江海。——荀子

名句故事

The quote is about doing things step by step. No man is born to be great. We have to work hard to become respectable. It is not a goal that we can achieve in a short time. It will take many years or even a whole lifetime.

We may aim high, but we have to bear in mind that an

ambitious goal cannot be accomplished at one stroke.

If you want to become a doctor, you must study hard to be admitted into a medical school. If you are not intellectually qualified, you just do not have any chance to become a doctor.

這句引言是在說循序漸進做事。沒有人生來就偉大，我們必須努力才能受人尊重，這不是短期之內就能達成的目標，要花許多年或甚至一輩子的時間才能達成。

我們可以把目標放遠，可是要記住遠大的目標不可能一蹴而成。

如果你想要成為一名醫師，你就得用功讀書進入醫學院就讀，如果在智能上無法符合資格，就沒有機會成為醫師。

句型文法解析

　　哲學名句有用到 step by step 這個片語，意思是一步一步或循序漸進，屬於副詞片語。

　　類似的片語還有 **little by little**、**inch by inch**、**bit by bit**、**stage by stage**、**by degrees**，也可以用副詞 gradually 或 progressively 來表示。

　　這類的副詞片語由三個英文字組成，中間是介系詞，前後則為名詞。結構相同，意思不同的片語有 **one by one**（一個一個地）、**day by day**（天天）、**face to face**（面對面）、**back to back**（背靠背）、**word for word**（逐字地）、**night after night**（夜夜）等。

　　比較常見的還是由兩個字構成的副詞片語，前一個字是介系詞，後一個字則為名詞或形容詞，at times（有時候）、in fact（事實上）、in haste（匆忙地）等屬於介系詞加上名詞組成的副詞片語。

　　at present（現在）、at last（最後）、in general（一般說來）等屬於介系詞加上形容詞構成的副詞片語。

　　既然是副詞片語，就要擺在句首或動詞的後面作為修飾之用。

英文例句

接著就來看看可以怎樣應用這類句型吧！

✡ **Step by step**, I have learned how to assemble a desktop computer. I can make a computer that best serves my needs.

我逐漸學會如何組合桌上型電腦，可以做出一台最符合我的需求的電腦。

✡ One by one, two Brothers Elephants players hit **back-to-back** home runs in the Elephants' game against the Eda Rhinos yesterday. They helped their team win the game.

兩位兄弟象隊球員在昨天與義大犀牛的比賽中連續擊出全壘打，幫助球隊贏得比賽。

✡ It is necessary to do things **step by step**, since nothing can be done at one stroke.

循序漸進做事有其必要，因為沒有任何事情可以一蹴而成。

3 ▶ much more / less

🏛 哲學名句

The indigo color is extracted from the indigo plant but excels the color of the plant that it comes from. Ice is made from water but is colder than water. ——*Hsun Tzu*

青取之於藍，而青於藍；冰，水為之，而寒於水。——荀子

📖 名句故事

What we can learn from the quote is that we can become better than our predecessors. We are reminded of a similar saying: "The waves behind ride on the waves before."

Figuratively speaking, it means that each new generation excels the previous one. It also indicates the constant evolution of all things.

Human beings are no exception. We must strive to become better than our predecessors, especially those in our office, so that we can contribute more to the company or organization that we work for.

It is not only for self-fulfillment, but also for the common good. As long as you are good enough, you do not have to worry about being replaced by someone better than you.

我們可以從這句引言學到，我們能比我們的前輩還棒。這讓我們想起一個類似的諺語：「長江後浪推前浪」。

比喻上來說，意思就是每個新世代都能勝過前一個世代，也象徵萬事萬物的不斷進化。

人類也不例外。我們必須努力超越我們的前輩，尤其是工作上的前輩，如此才能對自己所待的公司或組織做出更多的貢獻。

這不只是為了自我實現，也是為了公眾的利益。只要你夠好，就不用擔心被更優秀的人取代。

句型文法解析

根據本單元要介紹的文法概念，可以把哲學名句改寫為：The indigo color is much more purer than the indigo plant that it comes from. 意思和原句差不多，只是多加了 much more（更加）這兩個字。

這裡的 much more 是在修飾後面的形容詞 purer（pure 的比較級），後面也可以接副詞或名詞，後面接名詞時和 many more 的意思相近，但 **much more 要接不可數名詞，many more** 則接**數名詞**。

先來和 many more 做一區別，以下有幾個例子：

Some people don't like the TV show, but many more people enjoy watching it.（有些人不喜歡這個電視節目，可是喜歡看的人更多。）

We have much more work to do.（我們還有更多的工作要做。）

由這兩個例句可明顯看出最大的差別就在名詞的可數與不可數。修飾形容詞時就只能用 much more。

例如：

This watch is much more expensive than I thought.（這支錶比我想得貴了許多）

This house is decorated much more beautifully than a hotel.（這間房子裝潢得比飯店還漂亮）。

英文**例句**

接著就來看看可以怎樣應用這類句型吧！

✡ Henry usually works overtime two to three times a week because his workload is **much more than** he can handle.
亨利通常一星期加班兩到三次，因為他的工作量遠超過他所能負荷。

✡ The farmers produce **much more rice than** the market needs this year, so the government has to intervene to maintain the price of rice at a level acceptable to the farmers.
農夫今年生產的稻米量遠超過市場所需，所以政府必須介入來把稻米價格維持在農夫可接受的水平。

✡ Mrs. Wang asks her children to walk across the street **much more carefully**.
王太太要她的小孩過馬路時要更加小心。

4 ▶ let alone

哲學名句

The gentleman learns through his ears and mind. The learning spreads to the four limbs and is manifest in his demeanor. ——Hsun Tzu

君子之學也，入乎耳，箸乎心，布乎四體，形乎動靜。——荀子

名句故事

If you want to learn something, you start from listening. You need to listen to what others talk about. Keep what you have learned in mind.

If you really absorb some knowledge, you will behave in a way that reflects your inner self.

Your demeanor indicates how learned you are. It means that we must judge a person by his appearance or outward behavior. The English proverb "Don't judge a person by his appearance" does not apply here.

A gentleman is a man of knowledge. He is as good as his word. He is the kind of man that a country needs to be strong.

如果你想學點東西，要從聆聽開始。仔細聽別人在講什麼，把學到的東西記在心裡。

如果你真的吸收了一些知識，你的行為模式將反映出你的內在自我。

由你的行為可看出你有多少學問，這意味著我們要根據一個人的外表或行為來判定他是怎樣的人。英文諺語「勿以貌取人」在這裡並不適用。

君子是有知識之人，言行一致，國家要有這種人才能強大。

句型文法解析

按照哲學名句，我們可以做這樣的改寫：The gentleman is not a man who will forget what he has learned, let alone a man who will behave in an improper way.（君子不是一個會忘記所學知識的人，更不是會做出不恰當行為的人）。

句子用到 **let alone** 這個片語，意思是「更別提，更不用說」，功能為連接詞，通常要主要子句為否定句時才用得上這個連接詞，**let alone** 後面可接動詞或名詞。

與 let alone 意思相近的片語還有 to say nothing of、not to speak of、not to mention、much less，先來看一些例子：

He didn't have any money to buy a meal, let alone rent a house.

He didn't have any money to buy a meal, much less rent a house.

He didn't have any money to buy a meal, to say nothing of renting a house.（他連買飯的錢都沒有，更不用說租房子。）

這三個句子都是同樣的意思。

let alone 和 much less 後面要接原形動詞，因為相對等的動詞是主要子句裡的 to buy，不過 to say nothing of 後面就一定要接動名詞，完全是因為介系詞 of 的關係。

英文例句

接著就來看看可以怎樣應用這類句型吧！

✡ Peter does not watch television, **let alone** play video games. He spends most of his time on studying.

彼得不看電視，更不用説玩電動遊戲。他把大部分時間用在讀書上。

✡ The old man could not remember the address of his house, **let alone** his home telephone number. The police had to help him find his home.

這位老人不記得自己家的住址，更不用説家裡的電話。警察必須幫他找到家。

✡ We should not talk loudly in a public place, **let alone** shout or sing. Such behavior is improper. We should know better.

我們不應該在公眾場合大聲交談，更不用説喊叫或唱歌，這樣的行為不適當，我們應該明白事理。

4 老莊思想：

道可道，非常道

1 begin with / start with

哲學名句

A journey of a thousand miles begins with a single step.

——Lao Tzu

千里之行，始於足下。——老子

名句故事

The quote is from the Tao Te Ching, a Chinese classic text believed to be written by ancient Chinese philosopher Lao Tzu. It is also about doing things step by step. But it indicates something more.

Of course, each journey, be it long or short, begins with a single step. What matters is the first step.

It is the first step toward a long journey or an ambitious goal. Many people do not dare to take the first step, so they end up regretting. What makes a man become successful is the courage to take the first step toward a big goal.

這句引言出自中國經典名著《道德經》，據信是中國古代哲學家老子的作品。這句話也是有關循序漸進做事，但別有其他含意。

當然，每一趟旅行，不論是短是長，都始於最初的一步，重要的就是這第一步。

這第一步是邁向長途旅行或遠大目標的第一步，許多人不敢踏出第一步，最後只能活在懊悔之中。一個人之所以成功是因為有勇氣向遠大的目標邁出第一步。

句型文法解析

千里之行始於足下的「始於」就是 **begin with**，用 **start with** 也可以，意思都是一樣，都在表達「**以⋯作為開始**」。

先來看一些例子：

In Taiwan spring begins with March.（台灣的春季從三月開始。）

He began with an apology for what he did.（他首先為他所做的事道歉。）

In the analysis of Shakespeare's poems, it is necessary to begin with his sonnets.（在分析莎士比亞的詩作時，必得從他的十四行詩開始。）

begin with 和 **start with** 也可以拆開來用，就是在動詞和介系詞之間加入名詞。

例如：
how to start a speech with power（如何有力地開始一場演講）

start a book report with a question（以一個問題作為讀書報告的開頭）

另外，要注意 **to begin with** 是作為副詞片語的獨立不定詞片語，意思是「首先」。

例如：
To begin with, I don't like this speech.（首先，我不喜歡這場演講。）

To begin with, he is too young to do the job.（首先，他太年輕做不了這項工作。）

begin with 是片語動詞，to begin with 則是不定詞片語，一個是做動詞用，一個則是副詞。

英文例句

接著就來看看可以怎樣應用這類句型吧！

✡ The plan has some advantages. **To begin with**, it can save a lot of money for the company.

這個計畫有些優點。首先，可以為公司省下許多錢。

✡ Many people like to **begin a speech with** "Thank you for coming. I've really been looking forward to seeing you today."

許多人喜歡在演講的一開頭說，「感謝各位的來到，我非常期待今日與你們相見。」

✡ Learning begins with curiosity. But it is better to **begin with** some simple ideas. If you want to walk a long distance, you have to walk step by step.

學習始於好奇。但一開始先學些簡單的概念就行，如果想走得又長又遠，就要按部就班。

2 ▶ leave

哲學名句

A good deed leaves no trace. ——*Lao Tzu*

善行，無轍跡。——老子

名句故事

The quote is also from the Tao Te Ching written by Lao Tzu. It means that a person who does a good deed will not let it be known by too many people.

A real charitable man prefers to do good things for others anonymously. Those who like to talk about their donations to charity organizations might be trying to fish for fame.

In the Tao Te Ching, Lao Tzu also says, "What is a good man but a bad man's teacher. What is a bad man but a good man's responsibility?"

A good man does something good not for his personal reputation. He wants to be an example for a bad person.

這句引言也是來自老子所寫的《道德經》，意思是行善之人不會讓太多人知道他的善行。

一個真正的善人比較喜歡不具名地為他人做好事。喜歡談論自己捐了多少錢給慈善機構的人，或許只是為了沽名釣譽。

老子在《道德經》中還說：「故善人者，不善人之師；不善人者，善人之資」。

好人做好事不是為了個人名譽，而是要給壞人做一個榜樣。

句型文法解析

　　本單元介紹的不是一套文法概念，而是一個常用的動詞，一般英語教學只著重文法，對於單字的運用並沒有特別強調，殊不知單字才是英文的基礎。

　　哲學名句 A good deed leaves no trace. 用到 **leave** 這個動詞，**意思是「留下」**，按照字面上的意義，整句就是「善行不留下任何痕跡」。

　　leave 最常見的意思是「**離開**」，看起來很簡單，其實這個單字涵蓋了好幾種不同的意思及用法。

　　leave 除了作為一般動詞外，也具有使役動詞的功能，例如：

The sudden change left me speechless.（突然的改變使我啞口無言。）
這裡的 left（leave 的過去式）等於 made（make 的過去式）

You must leave your room locked.（你必須鎖住門。）

　　另外，leave 也具有授與動詞的功能，這類動詞最常見的有 give 和 buy，比較麻煩的部分是直接受詞和間接受詞的擺放位置，例如：

He left his wife a great fortune.

He left a great fortune to his wife. （他留下一大筆財富給老婆。）

句子裡的直接受詞是 a great fortune，間接受詞則為 his wife。

 **英文例句**

接著就來看看可以怎樣應用這類句型吧！

✨ She **left her boyfriend waiting** outside in the rain because she was angry with him for his failure to keep his promise.
她讓男朋友在外面淋著雨等，因為她氣他未能兌現承諾。

✨ The teacher's smile **leaves much room** for imagination. It might mean that the teacher has some good news for us.
老師的笑容留下許多的想像空間，可能表示他有好消息要告訴我們。

✨ It is not necessary **leave the door open**. Leave the door locked all the time to prevent a burglary from happening.
沒有必要開著門，門要隨時保持上鎖，以免遭到竊盜入侵。

3 ▶ 祈使句

|||| 哲學名句

Show plainness; embrace simplicity. Reduce selfishness; minimize desires. ——*Lao Tzu*

見素抱樸，少私寡欲。——老子

名句故事

A little like the Bible, the Tao Te Ching gives instructions on how to live a life.

Lao Tzu recommends a plain and simple life. The less selfish, the better. It is also necessary to have as few desires as possible.

Most of our problems stem from our failure to live a simple life. Having few or no desires is an important part of wu-wei (taking no action), which is one of the central ideas of Lao Tzu's philosophy.

Taking no action does not mean doing nothing at all. It means having no selfish desires. The only desire that we should have is to have no desires at all.

《道德經》有點類似《聖經》，都在指示如何過生活。

老子推薦樸實簡單的生活，越不自私越好，慾望越少越好。

我們的問題大多是因為未能過著簡單的生活，慾望很少或沒有慾望是「無為」這個概念的重要組成，而無為則是老子哲學的中心概念之一。

無為不代表不做任何事情，而是沒有私欲。我們該有的唯一慾望就是不要有任何慾望。

句型文法解析

哲學名句用到了祈使語氣，也就是把原形動詞置於句首，所表達的是：

1. 告知、要求某人做什麼

2. 提出建議、勸告、指示

3. 表達祝福

Show plainness.可以解釋為一種建議，也可以說成一種要求。

當老師說，"Please keep quiet."，就是在做要求，要求大家安靜下來。當你到某人家作客，主人對你說，"Have some tea."，就是請你喝茶，這個時候就不是命令，而是一種邀請。

雖然形式上一樣，但祈使句在不同的情境有不同的含意。否定祈使句通常是在表達要求，例如：

Please don't smoke here.（請不要在這裡抽煙。）

Never speak to me like that again!（不要再那樣對我講話！）

祈使句經常和 and 或 or 一起形成並列句，例如：

Shut up, or I'll report it to your parents.

If you don't shut up, I'll report it to your parents.

（閉嘴，不然我要給你的父母知道。）

Study hard and you'll pass the exam.

If you study hard, you'll pass the exam.
（用功讀書就能通過考試）。

接著就來看看可以怎樣應用這類句型吧！

※ **Stay calm** and you'll find that the problem is not as serious as you thought. You haven't tried you best.
保持冷靜，你就會發現問題沒想像的那麼嚴重。你還沒盡最大的努力。

※ **Behave yourself**, or you will be in trouble. **Do remember** that you are not a child anymore.
規矩一點，不然你會有麻煩。請記住你已不是小孩了。

※ **Get your job done** before you go out to have dinner with your friends. It is your responsibility. **Don't ask somebody else** to do it for you.
在出去和朋友吃晚餐前要把工作做完。那是你的責任，不要找別人來幫你做。

4 動名詞

川 哲學名句

Knowing others shows your intelligence; knowing yourself shows your true wisdom. Mastering others shows your strength; mastering yourself shows your true power.

——Lao Tzu

知人者智，自知者明；勝人者有力，自勝者強。——老子

名句故事

It is not difficult to understand others. A man with sufficient intelligence can do it. But only a man with true wisdom can understand himself.

As is often the case, people tend to live in self-deception. They think too much of themselves. It requires wisdom to see through self-deception.

In the same way, a man who is physically superior can show his strength by beating others on the battlefield or in sports contests. But he tends to misuse his strength and bully people who are not as strong as he. He has to learn how to master his strength before he can win the respect of others.

　　瞭解他人並不難，有足夠聰明才智的人都做得到。但只有擁有真正智慧的人才能認識自己。

　　經常的狀況是，人們傾向於活在自我欺騙之中。他們自視過高。要有智慧才能看穿自我欺騙。

　　同樣地，體格上優越的人可以藉著在戰場上或運動比賽中擊敗他人來展現自己的力量，可是卻容易誤用力量欺負比較弱小的人。這種人必須學習如何控制自己的力量，才能得到他人的尊重。

句型文法解析

哲學名句 Knowing others shows your strength.中的 knowing 是動名詞，和後面的受詞 others 構成了句子的主詞。

動名詞在形式上和動詞的現在分詞一樣，但主要是作為名詞之用。雖然詞性上是名詞，動名詞卻保有動詞的特性，像是後面可以接受詞，knowing others 即為一例。

動名詞可當主詞、補語、受詞、及介系詞的受詞，例如：
Reading books is a good hobby.（讀書是良好的嗜好。）
這裡的動名詞 reading books 就是主詞。

My favorite hobby is cooking.（我偏愛的嗜好是煮菜。）
這裡的動名詞 cooking 是主詞補語。

I enjoy playing tennis.（我喜歡打網球。）
這裡的動名詞 playing 是動詞 enjoy 的受詞。

She is good at writing.（她擅長寫作。）
這裡的動名詞 writing 是介系詞 at 的受詞。

He left without saying anything.（他沒說一句話就走了。）
這裡的動名詞 saying 是介系詞 without 的受詞。

動名詞也有被動語態和完成式，例如：

Nobody likes being ridiculed in public.（沒人喜歡被公開嘲笑。）

being ridiculed 就是被動語態的動名詞。

He is proud of having won a writing contest.（他對於贏過寫作比賽感到驕傲。）

having won 就是動名詞的完成式。

英文例句

接著就來看看可以怎樣應用這類句型吧！

✣ He **remembered having** seen the woman once before, but he was not sure of where he had seen her.

他記得曾經見過這位女子一次，但不確定在哪裡見過。

✣ Taiwan people **are proud of having** Wang Chien-ming as the first Taiwan baseball pitcher to get nearly 20 wins in a season of the U.S. Major League.

台灣人對於王建民成為第一位在美國大聯盟，拿到單季近 20 勝成績的台灣投手，感到驕傲。

✣ **Playing video games** can be fun, but it has some disadvantages. Play only in your leisure time.

玩電動遊戲很有趣，但也有些缺點。你只能在休閒時間玩這些遊戲。

5 if 的省略

 **哲學名句**

Making no claim to greatness leads to greatness.

——Lao Tzu

以其終不自為大，故能成其大。——老子

名句故事

A great man is not great because he calls himself great. He has to earn the recognition of others.

A really great man will not claim to be great. He prefers to keep a low profile. He does not take credit for the good deeds that he has done. He does not consider himself to be the benefactor of those who he has helped, nor does he ask for any return. That he makes no claim to greatness makes him become a great man.

By contrast, those who like to let their good deeds be known by as many people as possible are not really great men. They still deserve to be praised, however.

偉人不是因為自己稱自己為偉大就是偉大,他必須贏得他人的認同。

真正的偉人不會自稱偉大,他比較喜歡保持低調,不會為自己做的善行居功,不認為自己是別人的恩人,也不要求任何回報。他不以偉大自居,才是他之所以偉大的原因。

相對之下,喜歡讓自己的善行被越多人知道越好的人,就不是真正的偉人,不過他們還是值得讚揚。

句型文法解析

　　根據本單元要介紹的文法概念，哲學名句可以改寫為：Had he done the good deeds for the sake of his reputation, the respectable philanthropist would not have won the respect of so many people.（如果這位受人景仰的慈善家當初是為了自己的名譽才做了善事，就不會贏得這麼多人的敬重）。

　　這是一種省略了 if 的假設句，原來應該是：
If he had done the good deeds for the sake of his reputation, the respectable philanthropist would not have won the respect of so many people.
　　由於是與過去事實相反的假設，所以要用過去完成式。

　　與現在事實相反的假設，則要用簡單過去式，不過不管第幾人稱，用到 be 動詞時都要採用 be 動詞過去式的複數形式，即 were，例如：
Were I rich, I would buy a big house for my family.
If I were rich, I would buy a big house for my family.
（如果我有錢，我就會給自己的家人買一棟大房子）。

　　與過去事實相反的例子則有：Had I had enough money, I would have helped you.（如果當時我有足夠的錢，我就會幫你），這種話講了等於沒講，因為就是沒有幫到忙。

接著就來看看可以怎樣應用這類句型吧！

✡ <u>**Had he asked**</u>, I would have told him the truth. Fortunately, he didn't ask. So I didn't have to say anything.

如果他當時有問，我就會告訴他實情。還好他沒問，所以我也不用説什麼。

✡ <u>**Were I a bird,**</u> I could have a bird eye's view of the world. It would be like seeing the world from the top of a mountain.

如果我是一隻鳥，我就可以鳥瞰整個世界，就像是從山頂看整個世界一般。

✡ <u>**Were she here**</u>, she would ask you a lot of questions about why you didn't invite her to attend the meeting.

如果她在這裡，她就會針對你沒邀請她參加這場會議一事問一大堆問題。

6 ▶ wish

 哲學名句

Misfortune might be a blessing in disguise and in good fortune lurks calamity. ——*Lao Tzu*

禍兮福所倚，福兮禍所伏。——老子

名句故事

The quote tells us that misfortune and good fortune share an interdependent relationship with each other. Because of this relationship, good things and bad things are interchangeable.

In other words, misfortune can turn into good fortune and good fortune into misfortune.

Don't take it for granted that good fortune or misfortune will last forever. Good things that you experience in life might not necessarily mean good fortune to you if you don't know their value.

As some bad things happen to you, don't feel frustrated and think it is the end of the world. Your bad luck would go away sooner or later.

這句引言告訴我們，禍與福之間有著相互依存的關係。由於這種關係，好事和壞事可以相互交換。

換句話說，禍可以轉換成福，而福也可以轉換成禍。

不要認定福或禍會持續下去。你在生命中所經歷到的好事，不見得對你是福，如果你不曉得其價值的話。

碰到壞事時，不要感到挫折並認為世界末日來到，你的壞運遲早會走開。

句型文法解析

　　為了配合本單元介紹的文法概念，我們可以根據哲學名句衍生出這樣的句子：He wishes that he had the good fortune to avoid misfortune, but as misfortune comes, he has no choice but to face it.（他真希望他有可以避開惡運的好運，不過當惡運來臨時，他也只得面對），句子用到以 wish 所帶動的假設語氣。

　　wish 後面所接的 **that** 子句，是在表達一種無法實現的願望，和現在事實相反時用簡單過去式，**be** 動詞要用過去式的複數形式，即 **were**。

　　和過去事實相反時則用過去完成式，用法和前一單元介紹的假設語氣一樣。

　　舉例來說：
I wish I were taller.（我真希望能高一點。）

　　I wish I didn't have to work today.（我真希望今天不用工作。）

　　I wish she had told me the truth when I asked her last time.（我真希望上次問她時她有告訴我真相。）

　　I wish I had listened to my father's advice.（我真希望當時聽了父親的建議）。

要記住 wish 後面的子句一定要用假設語氣。

英文例句

接著就來看看可以怎樣應用這類句型吧！

✡ **She wishes she had won** the beauty contest. If she had won the contest, she would have got the chance to earn a lot of money.

她真希望當時能贏得選美比賽。如果贏了那場比賽，她將有機會賺很多錢。

✡ **He wishes he were** the mayor of Taipei. He wants to improve the traffic condition of the city.

他真希望自己是台北市長，他想要改善市區的交通狀況。

✡ **I wish I had been assigned** to a different department of the company. But I have got used to the current working environment.

我真希望當時被分派到公司的另一部門，可是我已經習慣了現在的工作環境。

1 ▶ suggest that...

III 哲學名句

Ultimate happiness is the absence of pursuing happiness,
and supreme honor is the absence of pursuing honor.
——*Chuang Tzu*

至樂無樂，至譽無譽。——莊子

名句故事

Everyone has the right to pursue happiness. But there are different kinds and levels of happiness.

Happiness at the first level is happiness from material objects. People get pleasure from owning things, such as a new car and a big house. This kind of happiness is often short-lived.

A higher level of happiness is from doing good for others. At this level, we care about other people and are no longer egoistic.

The highest level of happiness involves a search for fullness and perfection. It is not an active pursuit of happiness. It is rather a feeling of fullness that one can feel anywhere and anytime.

每人都有追求快樂的權利，可是快樂有不同的種類和層次。

第一層次的快樂是物質上的快樂，人們因為擁有新車或大房子之類的物品而感到快樂，不過這樣的快樂通常是短暫的。

較高一層的快樂是為他人做好事，達到這一層次的人會關心別人，不再以自我為中心。

最高層次的快樂包含了對完整和完美的追求，這不是主動地追求快樂，而是一種可以在任何地方和任何時間感受完整和充實的感覺。

句型文法解析

　　根據本單元要介紹的文法概念，我們可以把哲學名句改寫為：The master suggests that we should not deliberately pursue happiness. True happiness comes naturally to us.（大師建議我們不該刻意追求快樂，真正的快樂是自然而然地來到。）

　　句子用到 suggest 這個動詞，其後面的 that 子句要用 should+原形動詞，should 可以省略，但省略之後，原形動詞仍是原形動詞。

　　這類的「提議、要求」動詞除了 suggest 外，還有 **insist**（堅持）、**advise**（勸告）、**decide**（決定）、**demand**（要求）、**order**（命令）、**propose**（提議）、**recommend**（建議）、**request**（要求）等。

　　舉例來説：
She suggests that we (should) share the taxi fare.（她建議我們一起分擔計程車費。）

　　The doctor insisted that I (should) quit smoking.（醫生堅持要我戒煙。）

　　The teacher suggested that Paul (should) read more books.（老師建議保羅多讀一些書。）

老莊思想

The general demands that all the soldiers under his command (should) maintain discipline.（將軍要求他所指揮的士兵要維持紀律。）

活用這個句型的要訣就是把相關的動詞背好，因為規則都是一樣，只有動詞不一樣而已。

 英文例句

接著就來看看可以怎樣應用這類句型吧！

✡ The doctor **suggests that** I take more exercise or go on a diet to lose weight. Either way is difficult for a fat man like me.
醫生建議我用多運動或節食的方式來減重。不管用哪種方式，對我這個胖子來說都很困難。

✡ Regarding Henry's being late to work, the boss **insisted that** Henry be punished as an example to other employees.
關於亨利上班遲到一事，老闆堅持要處罰他，好讓其他員工有所警惕。

✡ The general manager **suggests that** employees who volunteer to work overtime be given a pay raise next year.
總經理建議明年給自願加班的員工加薪。

2 It is necessary / essential that...

🏛 哲學名句

Free your mind and follow the way of nature without leaving room for selfishness. The whole world will become orderly and peaceful by then. ——Chuang Tzu

游心於淡，合氣於漠，順物自然而無容私焉，而天下治矣。

——莊子

📖 名句故事

The world has so many problems mainly because of people's selfishness. A man can live a happier life if he knows how to free his mind.

Freeing one's mind means letting go of prejudice, selfishness and self-righteousness. The environment suffers so much damage because human beings exploit natural resources to satisfy their desires.

Human selfishness is the origin of all the world's problems. But humans are naturally selfish. It is impossible to eliminate selfishness. What we can do is to reduce our selfishness as much as we can. A man who can free his mind and see the world from a larger perspective tends not to be selfish.

世界有這麼多問題主要因為人們的自私。一個人只要知道如何釋放自己的心靈，就能過得更快樂。

釋放自己的心靈就是放掉自己的偏見、自私及自以為是。自然環境遭受這麼大的破壞，都是因為人類為了滿足自己的慾望不斷掠奪天然資源。

人類的自私是世界所有問題的來源，可是人類天生就自私，不可能完全消除自私，只能盡量減少自私。一個能夠釋放自己的心靈並用更大的觀點來看待這個世界的人，通常不會自私。

句型文法解析

上一單元介紹了 suggest 等「建議、要求」動詞後面接 that 子句的句型，本單元則要介紹類似的句型，即 **It is...t hat S should+原形動詞句型**，**It is** 後面接 **necessary** 和 **essential** 表示「必要」。

根據這個句型，哲學名句可以改寫為：It is necessary that you (should) free your mind and follow the way of nature.（你有必要釋放心靈並遵從自然之法），這個句型中 that 子句的 should 也是可以省略，但動詞還是要用原形動詞。

除了 necessary 和 essential 以外，important（重要的）、desirable（希望的）、urgent（緊急的）等也是這類句型常用的形容詞。

舉例來說：
It is necessary that you should turn in your report on time.（你有必要準時交報告。）

It is essential that you should take the medicine according to the doctor's instructions.（你絕對有必要按照醫生的指示服藥。）

It is important that students should respect their teachers.（學生尊敬老師是重要的。）

It is urgent that search and rescue efforts should start immediately after an earthquake.（地震後急需要立即展開搜救工作。）

🌾 **英文例句**

接著就來看看可以怎樣應用這類句型吧！

✡ **It is necessary that** you should take a test to qualify for the position. As long as you pass the test, you can get the job.
為了符合這個職位所需要的資格，你有必要接受測驗。只要通過測驗，你就可以得到工作。

✡ **It is essential that** a patient with high blood pressure should check his / her blood pressure several times a day.
高血壓病人絕對有必要每天量血壓好幾次。

✡ **It is important that** you should start preparing for the rainy day as early as possible.
你趁早未雨綢繆是重要的。

3 ▶ It is high / about time that...

|||| 哲學名句

The friendship between gentlemen is light like water; the friendship between amoral men is sweet like wine.

——Chuang Tzu

君子之交淡若水，小人之交甘若醴。——莊子

名句故事

The so-called gentlemen are men of virtue. They make friends with people with similar qualities. These virtuous people treat each other with respect, and they won't get together too often or too closely. As the saying goes, "Familiarity breeds contempt."

On the contrary, amoral men, men with a lowly character,

like to hang out together at places like night clubs where they gossip about other people. They don't treat each other with respect, which is the reason why their friendship usually doesn't last long.

Real friends won't care less about you just because you don't spend time with them. But such friends are not easy to find.

所謂的君子是指有德行之人，他們結交的都是與自己相似之人。這些有德行之人相互尊重，不會經常聚在一起，也不會過於親近。誠如俗諺所説：「親近則狎侮」。

反之，品格低下的小人喜歡聚集在夜總會之類的地點談論他人的是非，他們不會相互尊重，以致於無法讓交情維持長久。

真正的朋友不會因為你沒有和他們在一起而少關心你一點，但這樣的朋友不容易找到。

句型文法解析

　　根據本單元要介紹的句型，哲學名句可衍生出這樣的句子：It is time that you found a real friend. True friendship is light as water, not sweet like wine.（該是你找一個真正的朋友的時候，真正的友誼淡如水，而不是甘如酒。）這個句子用到 **It is (high / about) time + that** 子句這個句型，用來表達「時候到了，該做某事」的假設語氣。

　　句型中的 that 子句可以用簡單過去式，也可以用 should+原形動詞。

例如：

It is (high / about) time that he went home.

就等於 It is (high / about) time that he should go home.

意思是「該是他回家的時候了」。

也可以用不定詞片語的方式來表達，即 It is time for him to go home.

　　瞭解句型之間的轉換，不但有助於文法概念的增強，也有助於提升寫作能力。

　　常常聽人説，It is about time to leave.，就是這種句型，意思是該走了，可是還沒有走。其他常聽到例句還有：

It is high time that you stopped talking nonsense.（你該停止胡説八道了。）

It is about time that you started doing something.（你該開始

做點事了。）

that 子句的 that 都可以省略不用。

英文例句

接著就來看看可以怎樣應用這類句型吧！

✡ Tom is already 55. **It is high time that** he started saving more money for his retirement. His only son has his own family to take care of.

湯姆已經 55 歲了，該是他開始為退休生活存更多錢的時候。他唯一的兒子有他自己的家庭要養。

✡ **It is high time that** we got our car checked. It has been making a lot of noise for weeks.

該是我們把車子送去檢查的時候，幾個禮拜以來車子一直發出許多噪音。

✡ **It is about time that** you went to bed. Don't waste your time in watching television.

該是你上床的時候了，不要浪費時間在看電視上。

4 ◗ 與過去事實相反的假設語氣

哲學名句

Once upon a time, I, Chuang Tzu, dreamt that I was a butterfly flitting around. The dream was so real that I didn't know I was Chuang Tzu. Then suddenly I woke up to find I was Chuang Tzu. But I couldn't tell whether I was Chuang Tzu dreaming I was a butterfly, or I was a butterfly dreaming I was Chuang Tzu. ──*Chuang Tzu*

昔者莊周夢為蝴蝶，栩栩然蝴蝶也，自喻適志與！不知周也。俄然覺，則蘧蘧然周也。不知周之夢為蝴蝶與，蝴蝶之夢為周與？

──莊子

 名句**故事**

The quote is about a dream that seems so real that the person who dreams the dream wonders, once awake, if he is still in the dream or if he is in the real world. This raises a question about the reality of one's existence, which has much discussion in Western philosophy but not so much discussion in Chinese philosophy.

Chuang Tzu is one of the few Chinese philosophers who have enlightened people with their insights into the meaning of reality.

In this cyber age, we spend too much time immersing in the digital world. Some people might not be able to tell what is the real world and what is the cyber world.

這段引言是在説夢境可以真實到讓人在醒了之後依舊搞不清楚自己是還在作夢或已回到了真實世界，這引發人類存在之真實性的議論，西方哲學對此有著許多討論，但中國哲學卻沒有太多著墨。

莊子是中國少數能對現實存在提出真知灼見並啟發人心的哲學家。

在這個電腦世紀，我們花太多時間沈浸在數位世界，某些人或許

分不出什麼是真實世界什麼是電腦世界。

句型文法解析

　　莊周夢蝶這一典故頗適合假設語氣，根據原句可衍生出這樣的句子：If Chuang Tzu had been a butterfly dreaming that he was Chuang Tzu, he could have been caught by a human who was not in a dream.（如果莊子是一隻夢到自己是莊子的蝴蝶，他就有可能被一個沒有在作夢的人類抓到）

　　句子用到與過去事實相反的假設語氣，即 **If + S + 過去完成式, S + would / could / might / should + have + 動詞的過去分詞**。

　　與過去事實相反的假設語句在前面的 62 單元有介紹過，那是以 wish 所帶出的句型，是單一子句。

　　這裡的假設句型比較完整，有 if 所帶出的條件子句，也有主要子句。

　　舉例來說：
If I had left earlier, I would have caught the bus.（如果我早一點離開，就可以搭上巴士。）
　　既然是與過去事實相反，就表示既沒有早一點離開，也沒有搭上巴士。

She would have died if she had not taken the medicine.
（如果她沒有服藥，就會死去。）
事實上是死裡逃生。

英文**例句**

接著就來看看可以怎樣應用這類句型吧！

✡ **If you had run faster**, you could have won the race. You failed to run your best race mainly because you were not well-prepared.

如果你再跑快一點，就可能贏得比賽。你未能跑出最好的成績，主要是因為沒有準備好。

✡ **If the couple had checked** in at the airport half an hour earlier, they would not have missed their flight for Japan.

如果這對夫妻早半個小時到機場報到，他們就不會錯過飛往日本的班機。

✡ Mr. Wang would have been bankrupt **if his best friend had not lent** money to him in time.

如果王先生的最好朋友沒有即時借錢給他，他就會破產。

5 ▶ lest S should V

哲學名句

Everyone knows the use of usefulness, but no one knows the use of uselessness. ——*Chuang Tzu*

人皆知有用之用，而莫知無用之用也。——莊子

名句故事

"Following the way of nature" is the core of Zhuang Tzu's philosophy. All things in the world are valuable in and of themselves.

We all know the value of useful things. But few of us understand why useless things could be useful.

It is not so difficult to understand why, if we know how

useless stuff like our household waste can be recycled and become useful again.

Even people labeled as losers or useless men can be useful in one way or another as long as they are given a chance to help others. Just don't give up on those who are not considered to be useful.

「順物自然」是莊子哲學的中心思想。世界上萬事萬物都有其價值。

我們都知道有用事物的價值，可是很少人懂得為何無用之物會有用。

要瞭解其緣由也不是那麼困難，如果我們知道居家垃圾之類的無用東西是如何可以被循環使用再次變得有用。

即使是被貼上失敗者或無用之人標籤的人，只要讓他們有機會幫助別人，就能發揮某種用處。不要放棄那些不被視為有用的人。

句型文法解析

根據本單元要介紹的句型，哲學名句可以衍生出這樣的句子：We must know the value of all things, either useful or useless, lest they should be wasted.（我們必須知道所有事物的價值，不管它們是有用還是無用，以免白白浪費掉。）

句子用到 **lest + S + (should) + 原形動詞句型**，意思是「**以免、免得**」，should 在這裡的意思不是「應該」，而是「可能」，可以省略不用，但後面的動詞還是要維持原形動詞形式。

也可以用 for fear that 句型來表達和 lest 一樣的意思，但要留待下一單元才來介紹。

舉例來說：
Keep quiet lest (for fear that) you should disturb other people in the library.（保持安靜以免打擾到圖書館中其他人。）
意思和 Keep quiet so as not to disturb other people in the library.
Keep quiet so that you will not disturb other people in the library.
這兩個句子的意思一樣，可以相互替代使用。

in case + that 子句也和 lest 句型有類似的意思，例如：I'll buy an umbrella in case there should be rain.（我要買把傘以免碰到下雨）。

接著就來看看可以怎樣應用這類句型吧！

✡ We must be careful not to hate anyone **lest evil thoughts should** occupy our hearts.

我們必須小心不要去恨任何人，以免邪惡思想佔據我們的心靈。

✡ Regarding the labor strikes in recent months, the government must take action immediately **lest there should be** more strikes.

關於近幾個月來的勞工罷工事件，政府必須立即採取行動，以免出現更多的罷工事件。

✡ The security guard kept watching all night **lest a burglar should** break into the apartment building that he was guarding. He didn't take any rest until the end of his shift.

這位保全守衛整夜保持警戒以免有盜賊入侵他所負責守護的公寓大樓，他直到下班時結束才休息。

6 ▶ for fear that

⫿⫿⫿ 哲學名句

Get to work at sunrise and retire at sunset. Wander freely between heaven and earth and feel at ease at all times.

——Chuang Tzu

日出而作，日入而息，逍遙於天地之間，而心意自得。

——莊子

📖 名句故事

In ancient China, farmers got to work at sunrise and rested at sunset. So were other people, who didn't have the night life as we do now. At night, they gazed at stars feeling their connection with the sky.

Without having so many distractions as we do now, ancient

people spent much more time on gazing at the sky and contemplating the universe and the meaning of life.

In doing so, a philosopher like Chuang Tzu began to feel that he was wandering freely between heaven and earth without any sort of uneasiness in the mind. It was like being at one with the universe.

在古代中國，農夫日出而作日落而息，其他人也是如此，他們沒有像現在一樣的夜生活。他們在夜裡看著天上的星星時感受到與星空的連結。

古人沒有和我們一樣有這麼多的分心事物，他們花了許多時間在觀星，思考宇宙奧秘和生命的意義。

在這麼做的同時，莊子之類的哲學家就開始感受到自己是在天地之間自由自在地遨遊，心裡沒有任何的不安，好像與宇宙合為一體。

句型文法解析

前一個單元提到 **for fear that** 子句句型可以用來替代 lest + S + (should) + 原形動詞句型，所以哲學名句衍生出這樣的句子：To wake up at sunrise and get off work at sunset, Tom keeps the habit of constantly looking at his watch and checking the time for fear that he might lose track of time.（為了日出就起床日落就下班，湯姆習慣於經常看自己的手錶，唯恐忘了時間）。

for fear 後面的 **that** 子句，可以用 **should / might / may** 這幾個助動詞，不會只用 **should**，意思都是「可能」。相較之下，**lest** 後面的句子卻只能用 **should** 來表達「可能」之意。

除了 that 字句外，for fear 後面也可以接介系詞 of，of 後面再接名詞或動名詞，如果覺得用 that 子句太麻煩或容易因要考慮用那個助動詞而出錯，不妨改用 for fear of 比較保險。

例如：

Mr. Lin asked his wife to remind him to take the medicine for fear that he might forget about it.（林先生要他的太太提醒他吃藥，以免他忘了這件事。）

也可以改成 Mr. Lin asked his wife to remind him to take the medicine for fear of forgetting about it.

英文例句

接著就來看看可以怎樣應用這類句型吧！

✡ We bought a lot of instant noodles and cookies **for fear that** the typhoon would cause a power outage. Candles were also a necessity at a time like this.

唯恐颱風會造成停電，我們買了許多泡麵和餅乾。在這個時候，蠟燭也是一個必需品。

✡ The father stayed awake all night **for fear that** his son, who got a cold, might need his help.

父親整夜未眠，唯恐得了感冒的兒子會需要他的幫助。

✡ Despite the booming economy, the manager of the company asked his employees to be more careful **for fear that** a minor mistake might cause the company to lose some orders.

儘管經濟發展一片榮景，這間公司的經營者還是要求員工要更小心，唯恐小小的失誤會造成公司訂單的流失。

Learn Smart 078

英文文法沒這麼難：我靠哲學名句 找回學文法的勇氣！

作　　者	許貴運	
發 行 人	周瑞德	
執行總監	齊心瑀	
行銷經理	楊景輝	
企劃編輯	魏于婷	
執行編輯	陳韋佑	
封面構成	高鍾琪	

內頁構成	菩薩蠻數位文化有限公司
印　　製	大亞彩色印刷製版股份有限公司
初　　版	2017 年 4 月
定　　價	新台幣 369 元
出　　版	倍斯特出版事業有限公司
電　　話	(02) 2351-2007
傳　　真	(02) 2351-0887
地　　址	100 台北市中正區福州街 1 號 10 樓之 2
E - m a i l	best.books.service@gmail.com
網　　址	www.bestbookstw.com

港澳地區總經銷	泛華發行代理有限公司
地　　　　址	香港新界將軍澳工業邨駿昌街 7 號 2 樓
電　　　　話	(852) 2798-2323
傳　　　　真	(852) 2796-5471

國家圖書館出版品預行編目資料

英文文法沒這麼難：一句哲學名句
就能理解它！ / 許乃文著. -- 初版.
-- 臺北市 : 倍斯特, 2017.04 面 ;
公分. -- (Learn smart ;78)
ISBN978-986-94428-1-7(平裝)1.英
語 2.語法
　　805.16　　　　　　106002854